APPLY TOWERS

TOWERS

Made Powerful

Myra King

Sweet Cherry
Publishing

Sweet Cherry
Publishing

Published by Sweet Cherry Publishing Limited
Unit E, Vulcan Business Complex
Vulcan Road
Leicester, LE5 3EB
United Kingdom

www.sweetcherrypublishing.com

First published in the UK in 2015
ISBN: 978-1-78226-278-7

Illustrations © Creative Books
Illustrated by Subrata Mahajan
Cover design and illustration by Andrew Davis

Apley Towers: Made Powerful

Printed and bound by Thomson Press India Ltd.

For my mother, Renette King - the Queen in the blue dress. I still see you in the shadows.

"Beware; for I am fearless, and therefore powerful."
- Mary Shelley in *Frankenstein*

✥ One ✥

The horse sprang into a canter, kicking up dirt with his mighty hooves, his rider sitting firm in the saddle, seven horses following him.

"No! *You* have to make your horse canter, he mustn't play follow the leader. If he canters without your say so, pull him back to a trot," fourteen-year-old Kaela Willoughby's voice sliced through the heat of the day and rocketed across the ring.

The sun beat down on the riders, it was February; sweat coated their faces in long streams, cutting trails through the dust. Kaela put her hands behind her neck to protect it from the rays. She was hot and irritated: South African summers were exhausting. And having to explain the same thing ten times was starting to drain her.

"Okay, everybody bring your horses back to a trot."

Kaela rode at a stable named Apley Towers. From time

to time she was allowed to teach the beginners' class. Aside from actually riding the horse, this was her favourite thing to do. Except in the heat, when they weren't listening. Then she would rather run off into the savannah, and take her chances with the lions.

The beginners all slowed, Kaela let them trot around the ring once before giving them the command to canter. Shanaeda Mohamed, the most advanced of the beginners, led the herd. Kaela watched Shanaeda's firm leg move behind the girth and nudge Star into a canter. Even though Kaela had just told them not to do it, the other seven riders did nothing and let their horses play follow the leader.

"I'm going to have to make them each lead," Kaela said to herself, "Or throw the lot of them to the lions."

Although the girls had very strong legs and gripped well with their calf muscles, they bounced around in the saddle as though they were on a trampoline. They were holding themselves stiffly and were not in the motion of the horses. Kaela would have to talk to them after the class.

"They are very bouncy," a voice called.

Kaela turned to look at the person responsible for the voice. It was a girl, standing against the fence. She was dressed in full riding gear, with long blonde hair tied tightly behind her head. Kaela had never seen her before.

"Okay, halt," she ordered with a wave of her hand. "Well done, girls. Take the horses for a walk."

Kaela walked over to the gate and opened it for the

beginners; they lead their horses out in single file just as they had been taught. Kaela watched them ride at a slow walk around the ring, then disappear behind the stables. She then closed the gate and headed for the new girl. She noticed that this stranger was wearing a pair of horse riding sunglasses. This particular piece of equipment was designed for riders with blonde eyelashes to wear when riding in sunlight. Those with brown or black eyelashes had a competitive edge over their blonde colleagues, as the dark colour helped the lashes protect the eyes from the glare of the sun. Blonde riders usually relied on mascara to stop the sun's reflection. But some riders, usually the wealthier ones, used sunglasses that sat so snugly on their faces that they could not come off, even if the rider came off the horse. Why this girl was wearing these glasses when she wasn't even in the saddle was beyond Kaela. It seemed as though she was purposely showing off.

"They are very bouncy, you should sort that out before it becomes a habit," Sunglasses Girl said.

"They are beginners," Kaela defended.

"That's the best time to sort it out," the girl replied.

Kaela was usually quick to defend the little people – her tongue attacked without her brain's say so, but today Kaela couldn't even begin to string a sentence together. Perhaps it was because this was not really an attack on the little people, this was an attack on Kaela herself.

"I would prefer it if you did not scream their faults at them," Kaela said.

"And how would you prefer to do it?" the girl asked.

"Tell it to them later, under calmer conditions," Kaela defended.

"When they are already off the horse and can't do anything about it," Sunglasses Girl said curtly, with what seemed like a smile twitching at her lips.

Kaela had no idea what to say back to that; nobody had ever questioned her teaching before.

"Don't worry, from now on I won't bring attention to their faults," Sunglasses Girl said as she turned around and walked off, sunglasses glinting in the sunlight and long ponytail swishing from side to side. Kaela had no idea what to say or do. If the two had been queens arguing borders over a round table, Kaela would have just lost her kingdom.

"Aaaah! Oh man," a voice cried from the stables.

Kaela looked over at Beatrix King, her best friend, who was famous for carrying far too much, far too precariously. Right now she carried two full water buckets, despite the fact that one bucket was roughly her size. They both tumbled to the floor with a splash and Trixie leaned her head back, letting out a long groan.

"Hey Trixie-True, let me guess: you were carrying too little?" Kaela said to her friend as she walked over.

"Of course, a third one would have balanced me out," Trixie said, her brown eyes twinkling.

Kaela picked up a bucket and carried it back to the tap.

"Who's the girl with the sunglasses?" Kaela asked as she waited for the bucket to fill.

"There's a girl with sunglasses?" Trixie asked.

"Yes, some blonde girl who thinks she owns the place, she yell–"

"*YOU* have the reins, *YOU* tell the horse where to go! Next time watch where you are going!" a voice screamed from behind the stall. The voice belonged to Bella Matthews, the titled stable bully. She was yelling at one of the beginners. Kaela and Trixie watched the spectacle for a moment before a groom appeared to rectify the squabble.

"Anybody who wants to take over this place has to compete with Princess over there," Trixie said with a frown, motioning her head in the direction of Bella.

Bella and Trixie were old enemies.

The girls filled the buckets and took them back to the horses. Although Kaela tried to concentrate on Trixie's gossip about the White Feather brothers – mutual friends who lived in Canada, and the topic of Trixie's constant fascination – her mind kept returning to the scene she had just been part of. Sunglasses Girl had been right: the beginners couldn't do anything about their mistakes once they were off the horse. But Kaela had always been taught to end the lesson on a good note, it was better for both horse and rider. There was no point in stressing the girls out just before the lesson ended. The fact that she had not been able to even try to defend herself set Kaela's teeth on edge. Aside from Bella, nobody had ever attacked her; she had not been prepared for it.

As the girls rounded the corner, two horses stuck their heads out the stalls in greeting.

"Who are they?" Kaela asked in alarm, almost dropping the bucket for a second time.

There was a chestnut with big, gentle eyes. The horse was so tall and lean that it could only have been a Thoroughbred. The other horse was significantly shorter: a bay with small inquisitive eyes and ears that were far too big for the small head.

"They belong to the new girl," Trixie said.

"The new girl?" Sunglasses Girl, "*Both* of them belong to her?" Kaela asked.

"Yes, both of them are hers," Trixie said. She had already walked off.

So she has expensive glasses and two horses? Kaela thought, *the woman isn't short of money. Or the desire to show it off.*

Kaela followed her with a backwards glance towards the new horses.

"Watch out!"

Kaela turned in time to see herself walk straight into Bart Oberon, the son of the stable owner. Kaela tried to hold the bucket back, but it smacked against her legs, ricocheted and hit Bart, then came back and got her legs for a second time. By the time the bucket had calmed down, both parties were sopping wet from the waist down.

"I'm so sorry," Kaela said breathlessly.

11

"Now you owe me chocolate," Bart said with a mischievous smile.

"Whatever. If someone owed me chocolate every time they walked into me, this entire stable would owe me the contents of a chocolate factory."

"It's for getting me wet," Bart argued.

"Oh please, you were probably headed out to the pool anyway."

"Come on Kaela, you're going to be late for class," another rider said as he led his horse past them, "I've already tacked Quiet Fire for you."

"Thanks Russell, I really appreciate it," Kaela called to him.

Bart stared after the retreating boy and horse, "He tacked your horse for you?"

"He just likes to help out, he tacks everybody's horses if they don't have time," Kaela said.

"I think he likes you."

"Russell? No! Russell likes Trixie; he's just sucking up so I'll put in a good word for him. But I do anyway: I think they'd make such a great couple, but Trixie thinks she'll catch the plague from him."

Bart's brow knitted together in puzzlement, he opened his mouth to answer but his mother, Wendy, beat him with the words, "Come on, don't dawdle, you're going to be late for class."

Kaela looked down at the empty bucket.

"Don't worry, I'll fill it, go get Quiet Fire," Bart said, taking the bucket.

"Thanks," Kaela said and ran back up the stable to Quiet Fire's stall. The black horse stood at his water bucket licking the water, more to entertain himself than out of thirst.

"Hello my boy," Kaela called to him.

Quiet Fire was not actually Kaela's horse, he belonged to the stable, but as an intermediate and advanced horse, he usually only had two riders and Kaela just happened to be one of them.

To save time, Kaela adjusted the stirrups in the stall. There were two ways to do this, either on foot or horseback. Kaela preferred horseback, where she could sit comfortably in the saddle and measure the stirrup against her ankle. She had more luck than when measuring the stirrup leather against her arm; she almost always had to redo it. She was starting to believe that her arms were either longer or shorter than they were meant to be. When she was done, she grabbed her hard hat and shoved it on her head. As she was clipping the straps beneath her chin, Derrick, the head groom, walked past the stall. Kaela turned, grabbed Quiet Fire's bridle, and hurried out the stall.

"Why is the floor all wet?" she heard Derrick cry.

She practically ran the rest of the way.

❦ Two ❧

Kaela's wet jodhpurs were rubbing her skin raw; for the first time in her life she could not wait to get off a horse. The irritation was getting in the way of her riding – she was making silly mistakes. Her exasperation was also affecting Quiet Fire, who was nearly as on edge as she was.

"Kaela, control that horse," Wendy said for the third time, as Quiet Fire pulled out of formation *again*.

Jumping was even worse. Kaela usually excelled at jumping; it was without a doubt her greatest talent on horseback. Although it wasn't Quiet Fire's favourite thing to do, when he did jump, he was magnificent. They made a very good team … when he chose to jump. Kaela usually loved the challenge he presented, today she wanted to throttle him for it. He refused every jump, even nearly throwing her. Kaela was not in the state of mind to get him to cooperate.

"Kaela, Quiet Fire is just being stubborn, he is taking advantage of you," Wendy said.

Kaela knew that, she did not have to be told. Bad turned to terrible when Sunglasses Girl showed up to watch the show. Kaela automatically felt judged.

"Try him once more," Wendy called. She knocked the top pole from the jump and let it lie beneath the bars. Kaela groaned inwardly, she could feel Sunglasses Girl's laughing eyes boring into her.

"Okay Space Cowgirl, go for it," Wendy called.

Kaela groaned again, Wendy only called people by their nicknames when she was disappointed in them.

Kaela turned Quiet Fire in two tight circles. She always did this when he was misbehaving; it was a way to remind him that she was there and in charge. When she could feel that his attention was back on her, she pointed him towards the jump. He planted his front hooves firmly in the ground, pushed his ears forward and gave a short whinny. A very good sign.

This is it, this is it, Kaela thought to herself.

She nudged him with her heel and he sprang into a canter, Kaela tightened her grip with her calves and got into the motion of the gait. The jump got closer and closer, Kaela raised herself half an inch out of the saddle, leaned forward, gave Quiet Fire more rein, pushed her heels down and …
HUNG ON FOR HER LIFE!

Instead of rising in the air at the place he had been

taught, Quiet Fire continued cantering. Just before hitting the poles, he spun to his left. To keep from flying out of the saddle, Kaela wrapped her arms around his neck and squeezed tightly. Her right leg hit the jump with such force that the whole thing – poles and stand – came crashing down. A bolt of pain shot through her leg, rattling her bones. Blinking back tears of pain and shame, she quickly got control of Quiet Fire before he got it into his head that he was free to do mischief.

Kaela looked around to see who had witnessed her shameful attempt. The intermediates on horseback had to keep the horses moving so were not all that free to watch her, there were no spectators today, and Wendy was used to seeing this.

The only person left was Sunglasses Girl.

Kaela was just waiting for her to say something: "Well she wasn't bouncy, but aren't you meant to jump it?" or "just wait until she gets off the horse then tell her that you are meant to jump *over* the jump."

But Sunglasses Girl never said a word. This made Kaela nervous.

"Kaela, let's call it quits. The more you force him, the worse it's going to get," Wendy said. She had walked over to Quiet Fire and was now stroking him along his sleek, black neck, "Horses have bad days just like people, don't forget."

Kaela had not forgotten, but she knew her mount. He was not having a bad day, he was a mischievous little boy who took advantage of the fact that his rider was not in her element.

"I can't call it quits: if I don't get him to jump now he is going to get it in his head that if he is naughty, he can get away with it. You know how stubborn he is."

Wendy did know. It had taken her a year to get Quiet Fire out of the habit of spitting apple chunks at people after a nine-year-old Bart had taught the horse what entertaining things he could do with leftover pieces. Eventually it became a rule that Quiet Fire was not allowed to eat apples, they had to be substituted with potatoes. By the time he began eating apples again he gulped them down so quickly that there were never any pieces left. From then on, the riders had to do everything they could to stop him from getting ideas in his head.

"He has to jump," Kaela said.

"I'll jump him."

Kaela turned in time to see Sunglasses Girl climb through the fence and walk towards them. She groaned inwardly for the third time that day.

"Good idea, Angela, a different rider may help," Wendy said.

Angela? The thing has a name?

Kaela reluctantly dismounted and handed the reins to Angela. She noticed for the first time that the other girl was quite a deal taller than she was.

"You're going to have to readjust the stirrups," Kaela said.

"No, it's okay, I'll jump without them," Angela said.

"You are going to jump a three foot jump without stirrups?" Kaela asked.

"Native Americans used to do it all the time," she said as she prepared to mount.

"Well unlike them, you have to wear a hard hat," Wendy interrupted.

Kaela gloated at the expression on Angela's face: she looked as though Wendy had just insulted her riding skills.

"Kaela, lend her your hard hat please," Wendy said.

This time it was Angela's turn to gloat. Kaela ripped the hard hat off her head and pushed it towards Angela; she hoped it was full of sweat. Angela put the hard hat on, mounted Quiet Fire and trotted him over to the pops. Kaela laughed in disbelief. 'Pops', or combinations, were a series of jumps put one after another, ranging from two to four jumps. Kaela found it funny that she could not get Quiet Fire to go over one jump, yet Angela believed that she could get him to go over two. Kaela stood next to Wendy with her arms aggressively folded across her chest. She watched Angela bring Quiet Fire to a canter before turning him, pointing him in the right direction, and urging him on. Despite the fact that Angela had no stirrups, she had the perfect form. *More than perfect*, Kaela realised with horror. Even though there was a motion that the rider had to get into when cantering, it was nearly impossible not to lift out of the saddle. Even the top riders in the world lifted, just a fraction or so, out of the saddle at every bounce. But

Angela's seat was glued firmly down; she sat as though the horse was not even moving beneath her.

She'll be able to keep her seat when he refuses, Kaela thought, *too bad.*

But Quiet Fire did not refuse; he sailed over both pops without a hitch and even gladly joined the herd of horses trotting around the ring.

Kaela was in such shock she actually felt her jaw drop.

"Well done, Angela," Wendy called, "That's the lesson ladies and gentlemen, take the horses for an outride."

Angela brought Quiet Fire up to Kaela, who stood staring up at someone else on her horse.

"He's a great mount, is he yours?" Angela asked.

"No, he's a school horse, but I usually ride him," Kaela said, trying to keep cool. She wondered if Angela could actually see the steam coming out of her ears.

"He's wonderful, lots of spirit," Angela said and dismounted. She handed back the hard hat and walked off, sunglasses glinting in the sunlight and ponytail swishing from side to side.

Kaela was not in the mood for an outride. She wasn't sure she could handle what would happen when the other riders started asking questions. Instead, she loosened Quiet Fire's girth and walked him around the ring. He seemed to enjoy the attention. He kept licking her neck and nibbling on her ear. Eventually she was confident enough to let go of the reins. Quiet Fire walked unaided next to her, sometimes

checking her hands to see what goodies they held. She walked five times around the ring, and Quiet Fire walked next to her. She loved these moments with him, when it was just the two of them. She did not have to stand on ceremony for anyone, and neither did he. It was just the two of them quietly enjoying each other's company. Neither Quiet Fire nor Kaela noticed the blonde girl with sunglasses, who had stopped everything and stood watching them.

"Trixie, can I talk to you?"

Trixie's stomach dropped into the saddle. She *hated* that sentence.

Nodding, she dismounted and walked Slow-Moe over to Wendy.

"Have you thought about what direction to go in with concerns to riding?"

"Um … No, I haven't thought … I don't really know what you are talking about. Direction?"

Wendy laughed and patted Slow-Moe on his smooth, chestnut neck.

"I simply meant, are you wanting to focus more on dressage or jumping?"

"Oh, dressage, definitely. Jumping is …" how to say what she thought without being insulting?

Wendy raised her eyebrows.

Trixie thought of all the words that described jumping: *stupid, foolish, waste of time, for the little people.*

"Jumping is not for me," she finally said.

"I didn't think so. You have too much of a scientist brain: why fly when you can control how something separate from you moves? Is that right?"

Trixie nodded.

Wendy sighed and looked at the ring, "As it stands, you are the only rider besides Bella who is more interested in dressage than jumping. So as much as I would like to dedicate entire lessons to the two of you, the sad truth is that you are vastly outnumbered by the jumpers. I've been speaking to Bella, and she has agreed to my suggestions. How would you feel if, two lessons a week, I separated you two from the flock and taught you in your own lessons in one of the other rings?"

A lesson with just Bella? Oh, the horror!

"But how would that work?"

"Monday, Wednesday and Friday, you'll be with the class and I'll teach it, you will still be doing dressage but on a limited scale, as well as jumping and anything else I usually teach. Tuesday and Thursday, someone else will teach and I'll take you and Bella and we'll work on the dressage."

"Why though? Why not just leave us?"

"The rest of the class has their needs and ambitions covered in the regular class. Bella needs to progress so that she can go up to the next level, and she cannot progress until her dressage is up to scratch. And you are bored with jumping."

"And if I progress in dressage?"

"You would move up to the next level."

"Meaning I would ride with the advanced class?"

Wendy pursed her lips, "We'll judge when we get there. The advanced class are still far more advanced than you are. You would be at a serious – or dangerous – disadvantage if you moved up any time soon."

"What are the rest going to be working on when Bella and I are doing dressage?"

"Jumping."

Trixie looked at the jumps; they were set up so that you had to do a serpentine in order to get through the entire course. That had been the only part of the lesson she had enjoyed: serpentines were a favourite dressage move. She had actually wondered how much better the jumping course would have been without the jumps.

But was it worth two hours a week of just Bella for company?

It was like having to reach through stinging nettles to pluck a blackberry.

"Do I have to talk to Bella at any point in the lesson?"

"Not if you don't want to."

"Then we have a deal."

Kaela was not able to groom Quiet Fire after class as one of the advanced riders wanted to ride him in her lesson. Kaela decided to give Trixie a hand before she went home. Trixie's blonde hair was in complete disarray, tendrils stuck up at all angles. Kaela knew that Trixie didn't especially care about her own exterior as long as her horse sparkled. Slow-Moe was also a school horse that Trixie had adopted as her own. He was an old man who was far more stubborn than Quiet Fire could ever be. So stubborn, in fact, that Trixie was the only one in the history of Apley Towers that could get him to gallop. Kaela had only ridden him once, but just from that experience she knew that Slow-Moe was a credit to Trixie's riding ability. Before Kaela walked into Slow-Moe's stall, she caught a glimpse of a sleek, black car in the car park. She had never seen it before and its presence struck her as odd. As a rule, parents kept their fancy cars away from the stable. Fancy ended at the gate. In the car park there was dirt and dust: there were Jag, Storm and Loki, stable dogs that were as big as ponies; there was even a flock of geese who pecked at their own reflections; and the occasional runaway horse who kicked at whatever was in the way, be it a fence or a vehicle. Not to mention Jeremy, the stable donkey, who believed that everything was there for him to chew on, including side mirrors and windscreen wipers. Bringing a fancy car into the car park was like parking it in front of an oncoming bulldozer and hoping for the best. Kaela walked a bit closer to see who had been unfortunate enough to ignore the rule. It gave her quite a shock when she saw Angela get into the back seat.

"Maybe it's not her," Kaela whispered.

She turned on her heel and walked towards the ring where the advanced riders were – no Angela. It really had been her getting into the car then.

"That's odd," Kaela said to herself.

She hurried back to Slow-Moe's stall, let herself in, picked up a curry comb and filled her in friend in on what had just happened.

"You saw her ride, she could only be an advanced rider," Kaela counted the point on her finger after laying out the evidence.

"She jumped. You and I can jump too," Trixie answered.

"She hangs around the stable for no reason whatsoever."

"Or just to show off her knowledge and expensive sunglasses," Trixie retorted, grinning to herself.

"She leaves when it's the advanced class."

"Probably so that she won't have to answer questions about why she isn't riding," Trixie said.

"And she can get Quiet Fire to jump the pops," Kaela moaned.

"So can you," Trixie said from behind Slow-Moe.

Trixie was right, Kaela could get Quiet Fire to do what she wanted him to do, she just had to be in the right frame of mind. And today that was the last thing she was in. She had caught a glimpse of Quiet Fire giving Moira, his advanced rider, just as much trouble. When she asked him to do a piaffe, he had actually lifted his front hooves a good foot off the ground. It was a slight rear and Moira was not prepared for it. She would have fallen if she had not wrapped her arms around his neck. But after pulling him in a tight circle, Moira had him behaving. Kaela came to the conclusion that Quiet Fire was feeling particularly mischievous that day and was just pushing his riders to see where their boundaries stood. On any other day he would not have gotten away with half as much as he did with Kaela.

"So what's the verdict?" Kaela asked her friend.

"A show-off. She has two horses she doesn't even seem to ride. She wears riding sunglasses when she is not on the horse. She has to be told to put a hard hat on. She does not use stirrups when even the greatest riders in the world use stirrups. And lastly, she yells at the Fairies for being bouncy when they've just started cantering. What does she expect, for them to be glued to the saddle like she is?" Trixie said, waving the curry comb with each point.

Kaela had forgotten about Angela yelling at the Fairies. 'Fairies' was the official nickname for the beginners. Wendy said they were called Fairies because 'beginners' is such a long word. Kaela believed that they were called Fairies because they were just so small and generally covered in sparkles. Most of them were half her size and still liked to put glittery stickers on everything they came across (including their poor horses). Therefore they needed defending against any bully, especially ones with riding sunglasses.

"Maybe it's all just a lie, maybe she can't ride at all, maybe … OUCH!"

Slow-Moe had used his big teeth to take a swipe at the waving curry comb, but had missed and bitten Trixie's thumb instead.

"You're right," Kaela said through peals of laughter, "It's all a lie. She can't really ride: she didn't *really* jump those three foot jumps without stirrups."

"So then why isn't she riding now?" Trixie asked.

Kaela had no answer.

Trixie didn't feel like going home just yet. She had cycled to the stable and was therefore able to leave whenever she felt like it. The rule in her house was that she had to be at home before sunset. She took advantage of this as much as possible. The girls had moved over to another horse in need of grooming. Liquorice was a privately owned horse, but the private owner had fallen and broken her ankle. Now the stable had come together to help keep her horse clean and exercised. Liquorice was without a doubt one of Trixie's favourite horses. He was an Arabian; he cost more than most people's houses. He was a beautiful combination of bay and black with a perfect star on his forehead. If he weren't a fierce competitor in the highest of South Africa's riding competitions, he would have been the perfect school horse. He was kind and gentle, and never misbehaved when he wasn't supposed to.

"Hey Liquorice old boy, how are you today?" Trixie asked as she walked up to him. He turned his head and sneezed on her, "Yes, I missed you too."

Kaela giggled, "You're having a bad day too – first being bitten, then being sneezed on. I am not sure I want to know what's next!"

"Hopefully nothing," Trixie frowned and began brushing the dust out of Liquorice's coat.

It was getting close to feeding time at the stable, all the grooms walked around collecting feeding buckets. When the groom came to Liquorice's stall, Kaela hauled the bucket over the door and handed it to him.

"Thanks a lot. Be good to him, he's had a rough day," the groom said, pointing to Liquorice.

"Why, what happened?" Trixie asked.

"He was put in KaPoe's stall while Joseph was mucking out his stall. When Bella saw that he was in *her* horse's stall, she threw one of her temper tantrums and poor Liquorice got the brunt of the blast," the groom said, shaking his head.

"Typical Bella. She yelled at the Fairies today too. I wish Liquorice had kicked her," Trixie said.

"I wish the Fairies would kick her," the groom said and walked off.

"Why is that girl so horrible?" Trixie asked as she rubbed Liquorice down.

"I don't know, maybe–"

"Hi girls," Wendy interrupted from the doorway, "You just reminded me – would one of you mind coming early tomorrow to give Liquorice a good exercise? I won't be around to do it."

"Why aren't you teaching the class?" Kaela asked in shock.

"Derrick is teaching so that I can sort out the feed."

"What is it? Opposite day? When have you ever had to sort the feed? Derrick does it. Now Derrick is doing your job so that you can do his job?" Kaela stopped for breath. "I think I need to go back to bed."

"Perhaps you do. Can one of you ride Liquorice for me tomorrow then?" Wendy raised her eyebrows.

"Sure, I'll ride him tomorrow," Trixie said.

"Thanks Trix," Wendy said, and turned around to leave.

"Wait," Kaela called, Wendy turned back to face them, "Why doesn't Angela ride in the advanced class?"

"Because she is more advanced than the class. She has private lessons in the mornings."

Kaela's shoulders slumped, "She is more *advanced* than the advanced riding class? She takes *private* lessons?"

"Yes," Wendy said and walked in the direction of the feed room.

Kaela turned towards Liquorice and Trixie, but her eyes were far away.

"Sunglasses Girl is more advanced than the advanced class?"

"Apparently," Trixie said. It didn't surprise her really. The way Angela took those pops without stirrups had to have meant that she was above and beyond the simpler things they were taught at Apley.

"Okay," Kaela said finally, pulling the curry comb out of Liquorice's coat, "Then why doesn't she go to school?"

"Because she is an alien sent to penetrate the very core of the stable, in order to bring it down," Trixie replied seriously.

"One day, someone is going to take you out for your backchat."

"Until that day, we have school and homework. We need to be on our way."

"Peter Pan never had to deal with any of this."

"No, but the dude did have to sword fight Captain Hook."

"I don't know which is worse."

Trixie stopped to think for just a second.

"Homework."

∽ Three ∾

Trixie stared in wonder at the laptop screen. A mix of apprehension, sadness and utter bewilderment filled her.

"Isn't she magnificent?" the voice from the video clip said.

Yes she is, Trixie thought, *yes she was.*

"And that's the end of it," an English voice said, "but has she done it again?"

Trixie held her breath, waiting for the judges to score the rider.

"And she has done it again! Tens across the board. A perfect score! Felicity Willoughby has done it again. First it was gold in the European Dressage Finals, and now gold in the Empire Games. Felicity Willoughby is unstoppable."

Trixie watched as the rider took a victory lap around the dressage ring, patting her black horse and waving to the crowds. Trixie fought the impulse to clap along with those crowds.

The clip quickly changed to another high profile dressage competition. This time, Felicity was dressed in an old-fashioned blue dress that was popular with noble women in the Victorian age. It was called a riding habit. It hung down the side of her black horse like a wing.

Felicity wore such an eye-catching outfit simply because she knew it would bring her more attention to ride in it (and she was never one to be tied down by mundane uniforms). After this particular Empire Games ride, the demand for habits had gone through the roof. Felicity was an odd combination – a serious horse rider as well as a fashion starter. You didn't see many of those around. She had also added drama to her magnificent ride by using a side saddle (there had been no subsequent demand for those), with her hair clipped up in curls that sat under a sweet little velvet cap, which trailed black lace over her shoulder. Felicity looked as though she could have ridden with Queen Victoria. This was the dressage competition that put Felicity Willoughby into the history books. She was the only female, the only South African and the only one with a stallion in the contest, yet her finished score was nearly double that of the man who came in second place. The fact that she did it all in a Victorian riding habit, high-heeled boots and riding a side saddle, blew the crowd away. She was the international dressage favourite from that point on. She probably still was, despite the fact that she hadn't competed in nearly ten years.

Trixie watched in amazed admiration as Felicity finished

the course, scored a near perfect round and left the ring without so much as smile. Once out of view of the crowds and judges, but not the cameras, she threw her crop on the floor, hopped out of the saddle, and flew into her husband's arms. He held her while she wept.

She had won. She had put both female and South African riders on the map. She had conquered the world. She had made herself immortal.

And she knew it.

"Wow! She was amazing," Trixie said with stars in her eyes.

The video changed to the winner's platform with some aristocrat Trixie had never heard of presenting the medals. In his achingly perfect English accent, he addressed the crowds, "Today I am proud to stand before you at the Empire Games. Although it is a competition between the best of the best, the Empire Games is also about unity. We – countries with nothing in common, with nothing to bind us, with oceans and continents between us – stand together. Today we celebrate not only our athletes, we celebrate our differences … and we celebrate each other. I am proud to present to these fine horsemen … Oops, and this amazing horsewoman, the medals of the Empire Games."

Trixie watched him place the bronze and silver medals on the necks of the men from Australia and New Zealand, and nervously put the gold medal over Felicity's head without touching her. A bit of black lace brushed his finger, and the duke backed away so quickly he nearly fell. Once he had regained composure, he addressed the crowd again, "What a day it is to be part of our illustrious community of countries, where our differences are our strengths and our tolerance and willingness to learn from each other is what makes us great. Ladies and Gentlemen, I present to you the dressage winners of the Empire Games."

The crowd went wild. But the camera focused on only one person. Felicity stared out bravely, her blue eyes were daggers of ambition. To her, the Empire Games was just one more rung on the ladder of success.

The video changed again, only this time there was no dressage ring, no black stallion, no Felicity.

A sombre reporter stood in front of the camera, a dark green landscape behind her.

"Police have officially called off the investigation. Her body has not been found but, after three weeks, the likelihood of finding the famed equestrian alive is extremely remote."

The image changed to a picture of Felicity in her blue Victorian riding habit with her gold medal around her neck.

"Felicity Willoughby was reported missing three weeks ago. According to her husband and mother-in-law, she took her horse, Black Satin, for a ride on the family farm. She hadn't returned by dark. The family and neighbours formed a search party but had to turn back when the weather changed for the worse. The next morning, police found Black Satin wandering around the western part of the farm. Black Satin appeared to have no wounds or any noticeable marks, leading police to believe that Felicity Willoughby fell from her horse, and that something startled him into abandoning her. A rescue mission was launched, headed up by police and backed by family, friends and local townspeople. Ms Willoughby's body was not found despite this extensive search. The rescue mission has been called off and, in a statement made this morning, the police commissioner has stated that the investigation has ended. The Willoughby family have asked for privacy at this very distressing time."

The scene changed to Felicity and Black Satin at the European Dressage Finals.

"Ms Willoughby has been famed for her daring attitude to both riding and competitions. She is the number one dressage rider in the world, and the only female champion to have won gold on a stallion. There is much stigma surrounding the use of stallions as they can be unpredictable and often dangerous. Ms Willoughby maintained that Black Satin would never put her in any sort of danger."

The clip changed to a man, broken by reality; dark clouds above his head; lost to heartbreak. And beside him, a little brunette girl.

"She leaves behind her a husband and a daughter named Kaela."

Trixie stared at the five-year-old version of her best friend. Tears welled in her eyes. She quickly skipped it to the next clip.

Felicity, in her Victorian dress, smiled at an interviewer after winning gold.

"And what is next for the champion team?" he asked into a microphone.

Felicity touched her stomach, "My next adventure is motherhood."

The crowd went wild.

"I hope I have a little girl who will ride big horses and win more gold in dressage than me."

Well, she was right about the first two.

Kaela would never compete in dressage. She always said that she hated it with the fire of a thousand suns.

"Hey, Mom," Trixie called, "Do you think of Kaela as an adopted daughter?"

"Of course," her mother said.

Well, if Trixie's mother thought that about Kaela, then it was safe to assume that Kaela's mother would have thought that about Trixie.

"I'll win those golds for you," she said.

On the screen, Felicity smiled at the camera.

"Hello Wawa, how was riding?" Leo Willoughby asked as Kaela walked through the door.

"Hi Dad, it was good; Quiet Fire was full of mischief though."

Kaela sat down on her couch. She had been given her own couch, covered in plastic so that no matter how dirty she was, she couldn't ruin it.

She closed her eyes for a second and let her surroundings fill her: the scent of her father – medicinal yet with a hint of wonder – mingled with that of the woman who sat on the other side of the lounge. Kaela opened her eyes and stared at the beauty snuggled into the black couch with a tray of vegetables on her lap. Four triangular pots sat on a butler's tray next to her. Every few seconds she would throw a sliced vegetable in. The routine was like a magic trick. Chop the carrot, throw the slice – ladies and gentleman, watch as I make this entire root vegetable disappear. Her grandmother had always fascinated her.

Alice Darling had shouldered the loss of her eldest daughter far better than any other member of Kaela's family had. After seeing how badly her son-in-law and granddaughter were struggling with a life devoid of Felicity, she had quickly moved in to help raise the lonely child and care for the wayward widower. She had been there ever since. Kaela admired her for her strength, for her sacrifice, for her love and devotion. But also simply because she was the mother of her mother – and that deserved every ounce of respect. Alice looked up and smiled, she knew Kaela loved the magic trick of the disappearing vegetables.

She smiled back, she knew Alice loved her smile.

"How was school?" Alice asked.

"The same boring old nonsense handed to us as though it was new."

"I'm sure it wasn't that bad," Leo said as he tried to find a decent channel to watch.

"It was … Do you know what we were told in 'health' today?" Kaela made the symbol of inverted commas at the word 'health'. She knew this would get her dad's attention.

"What commercial drivel were you told?"

"That cow's milk is nature's most perfect food. Yeah, if you are a calf maybe. As a human, it is far from perfect for me."

Leo – the homeopath and purveyor of natural medicine and holistic health – smiled at his daughter, "You make me so proud. I feel like I don't even have to teach you things any more. You know all there is to know already."

"You can teach me how to argue."

"You are pretty good at that already," Alice said with big eyes.

"No, seriously. When I told the 'health' teacher that milk is only that good for you if you are a cow, she refused to listen to anything I had to say. If I was better at arguing, she would have listened to me."

Leo smiled at his only child, "Have you ever heard the saying, 'Once I was smart and so I tried to change the world, now I am wise and I only try to change myself'? Let her believe whatever she wants to believe: as long as you know the truth, what does it matter?"

"She is teaching lies."

"And the only way anyone would know that is if they went and discovered it for themselves. The truth is only for those who look for it."

Kaela gave up the argument, she knew she could never convince her father that screaming the truth of matters was better than his way. Instead she took off her chaps. The feeling of blood flowing freely through her calves startled her. She hadn't even realised there had been a restriction. She looked at her chaps and realised, for the first time, that they were too small.

"I think I have outgrown my chaps," Kaela said.

"How long have you had them?" Leo asked.

"Since I was ten," Kaela said, having to think for only a moment.

"Well four years is a long time for something to last. We'll go buy new ones on the weekend, you can give those chaps to a charity," Alice said.

The memory of school had brought other memories too.

"Dad, do people my age have to go to school?"

"Yes, it is against the law not to send children to school."

"But what if I know a girl who doesn't go to school?" Kaela asked.

"She is probably homeschooled," Alice said.

Kaela thumped back against the couch; wasn't Sunglasses Girl just so full of surprises?

Kaela quickly logged into the social media site, LetsChat, and found the name of her friend, Phoenix White Feather. She clicked on it, waited for Phoenix's page to load and clicked on the 'Chat' button.

Kaela: There is this new girl at the stable. She is totally mean. I barely know her and I totally wanna throw her into the Indian Ocean.

Phoenix: I can tell, you have lost your grasp of the vernacular.

Kaela laughed and rolled her eyes. The two girls had never actually met. They had found each other on LetsChat in a group called *The Writer's Den*. Where Kaela hoped to achieve immortality with bestselling books, Phoenix wished to see her name up on Broadway as an award-winning playwright. The two, along with Trixie, had formed an invite-only club called *The Lost Kodas*. A group made for the wayward teens to support one another in all things.

Kaela: True. Seriously though, she is utterly rude. She insulted the beginners. They are seven and eight years old. And she insulted them.

Phoenix: What did she say?

Kaela: She saw them cantering and said they were bouncy.

Phoenix: Were they?

Kaela: Yes.

Phoenix: I fail to see the problem.

Kaela: You don't tell someone they are bouncy.

Phoenix: But then how will they improve?

Kaela slumped back into the chair. Was she the only one to see sense? Why did no one else think this was wrong?

Kaela: You are supposed to end the lesson on a good note. Not on a 'Hey you there! Yeah, you! You are bouncy, that is all' note. Work with it next time.

Phoenix: I see your point.

Kaela: Good.

Phoenix: But I also see hers.

Kaela tossed her head angrily, the world was mad today. No one wanted to see her side of things. No one wanted to agree with her.

She needed to change the subject.

Kaela: And then she said 'Native Americans jump without stirrups'.

Phoenix: They do.

Kaela: I KNOW! But she isn't allowed to say it.

Phoenix: Why not?

Kaela: Because she doesn't have Native American friends, only I do.

Phoenix: Are you looking for reasons to hate her now? And anyway, I'm a First Nations woman. Canada, remember!

Kaela: Well, you know what I mean! And no, of course I'm not. She is just so annoying.

Phoenix: I can tell. Maybe you need a glass of warm milk and a long sleep.

Kaela: NO MILK!!!!!!!!!!!!

❧ Four ❧

Trixie, feeling rather daring and grown up, hopped into the taxi and gave the driver the address of Apley Towers.

"I know it," he said, "My daughter used to ride there before she discovered boys."

"You should tell her we have boy horses, she could have stayed."

The driver laughed and pulled away from the school gates.

Trixie smiled at the success of her joke: she was conquering the world – soon enough she would be wearing her own blue riding habit!

For what was more than likely the billionth time, she checked her blazer pocket to make sure her mother's money was still there. It was. She breathed a sigh of relief; she didn't want to know what would happen if a taxi took you somewhere and you had no money to pay.

She quickly grabbed her mobile and phoned her mother, who answered after only one ring.

"Hi Mom. I'm in the taxi. We are almost there."

"Okay, thanks for letting me know, I'll pick you up when I've finished work."

"Sounds good!"

She bid her mother goodbye and disconnected the call.

"Is she one of those helicopter mothers?" the driver asked.

Trixie had no idea what a 'helicopter mother' was but it didn't sound particularly appealing.

"No, she is not. I need to get to the stable early and she couldn't fetch me from school. So, she booked me a taxi and gave me money for it."

"Lucky for me, huh?" the driver asked as he pulled up alongside Apley Towers and stopped just before the gate.

Yes, he knew Apley all right. He knew not to bring the car anywhere near the car park or Jeremy.

Trixie paid, thanked him and hopped out. She quickly ran to the tack room which had an adjoining bathroom, rushed in and locked the door. She changed into her riding gear as quickly as possible. Once she was done, she stashed her school bag and uniform in the corner of the room. She then grabbed Liquorice's equipment and raced off to tack him.

Technically, she didn't need to race as there were nearly two hours before her own class, but she wanted to get in as much riding time as possible. Both she and Liquorice needed it.

She hadn't wanted to say anything to Wendy, but she was actually rather nervous about these private lessons. Being alone with Bella might break her concentration or worse, prove that she was behind Bella in terms of skill. Not to mention, dressage was *her* thing. She had to be good at it or nobody would take her seriously.

She needed as much practice with a dressage horse as possible.

Luckily for her, Liquorice was as eager to get into the ring as she was. He seemed to be helping her to get his tack on. At the sight of the saddle, he angled his back so that she could put it on. He even seemed to be stretching his neck in order to get the bit in his mouth before Trixie was ready.

"Okay boy," Trixie said as soon as they were both fully equipped, "Let's do this."

She gave Liquorice a quick pat on the neck, led him to the advanced ring and mounted. He was a lot smaller than Slow-Moe and, being used to the massive hop that was required to get up into his saddle, Trixie nearly propelled herself right over his back.

Jeremy began hee-hawing at her.

"Oh go laugh at your reflection, you creep," she said to him as she settled into the saddle.

She measured the stirrups against her ankle; they were far too long. She pulled back the saddle flap and grabbed the stirrup leather. She unclipped the buckle and pulled the leather towards herself until the stirrup sat against her ankle.

She redid the buckle and moved onto the next one.

"If you were any sort of a genius you would have done this on the ground," Trixie lectured herself.

She had always hated measuring the stirrups from the saddle, it was easier on the ground.

"Okay, done. Are you ready Liquorice?"

At the mention of his name, he swivelled his ears around.

"Well, let's go."

Trixie had memorised one of Felicity's more simple dressage routines and planned to spend the next hour practising that.

"I apologise for how simple this dressage routine is, Liquorice, I know you are used to more difficult stuff. Don't worry, there is one difficult move to do – a counter-canter – but I know you've done a ton of those too. Which is good, because I haven't."

With that, she nudged Liquorice into a walk, and took the first steps of her dressage career.

Kaela arrived at the stable with plans for a good day: she would teach the first class the way she wanted to teach them, and would ride like she usually rode. No wet jodhpurs, no embarrassing jumping mishaps, and certainly no run-ins with the new girl. It was going to be a good day.

And it was a good day until Kaela laid eyes on the

beginners' riding ring. Seven little girls on horseback trotted around the ring while a blonde girl with sunglasses stood in the middle directing them.

"Wha–"

Kaela ran off to find somebody. Anybody. The great Oz behind the curtain; the Cheshire Cat; Peter Pan; Bluebeard …! At this point she would take an explanation from Captain Hook. She encountered Joseph mucking the stalls, his face creased in concentration. It erupted into a grin when he saw Kaela.

"Miss Willoughby, what can I do for you today?" Joseph asked, his white teeth sparkling.

"Why is the beginners' class early?"

"Early?" Concentration was replaced by confusion.

"Yes, it's not time for class yet, but Angela is already teaching it," Kaela said, she was holding her breath to stop herself from screaming.

"But it is time for class, it's been time for class for a good twenty minutes," Joseph said.

Kaela looked at her watch, it was quarter past two. It had been quarter past two the last time she looked at her watch. And, she now remembered, the time before that as well. She looked closely and saw that the red second hand had stopped.

"No! What's the proper time?" she asked with a sigh.

Joseph pushed his sleeve back, and stared at his watch, "It has just gone twenty-five past three."

Twenty-five past three? The class had already been going for twenty-five minutes.

"Thank you Joseph."

He tipped an imaginary hat to her and went about his mucking.

She walked with lead feet past the stables and towards the riding ring; Angela had the riders drop their stirrups. Kaela was glad to see that their legs had progressed to such a point that they were able to post without stirrups. She felt herself swell up with pride.

Kaela sat watching the class for fifteen minutes; from where she sat she could also watch Trixie exercising Liquorice. Kaela's eyes swept over the body of her friend: the only mistake she could find was Trixie's elbows. Trixie never remembered to bend her elbows, but where it would have affected anybody else's riding, Trixie was able to ride perfectly. She had Liquorice at a counter-canter – an extremely difficult and complicated dressage move. Liquorice was something of a push-button horse – he would do anything you asked of him. So, doing a complicated move was exceptionally easy. Kaela's eyes darted back and forth over both scenes. In one, Angela was usurping her, in the other, Trixie was riding at a level beyond what was expected of them.

Hot, black jealousy lifted from the depths of her. Anger bled all over her heart. She ground her teeth and squared her eyes at both girls.

"Do you know what I've noticed about jealousy?" Joseph

said as he walked past, "Its enemy is laughter. Isn't that interesting?"

"Everybody, prepare to canter," Angela's voice entered Kaela's ears, breaking her confusion over Joseph's obscure sentence.

Kirsten, Bella's little sister, led the troops today. Kaela could see her tightening her grip on the horse and settling further into the saddle.

"And … canter."

Kirsten nudged Flight into a canter, he easily fell into the motion and so did she. Unfortunately, the six horses behind Flight sprang into action without being told to do so. They were once again playing follow the leader. Kaela laughed long and hard, more from relief than at the horses.

So Sunglasses Girl might not be good at *everything*.

When Kaela had finally settled down, she felt light and serene.

Joseph was right: the enemy of jealousy was laughter.

"That was amazing! It was unbelievable! Maybe I should ride horses that are trained specifically for dressage," Trixie said as she untacked Liquorice.

"Get a stallion, they are the best dressage horses around," Angela said as she walked past.

Trixie thought of the video of Felicity Willoughby's news

report. Black Satin had been a stallion. Had that been the reason for her death?

As far as Trixie knew, she'd never ridden a stallion. There were none at Apley, they were considered too dangerous.

Had Felicity Willoughby been playing with death whenever she had sat in the saddle? Had death finally won?

Maybe death walked amongst us as a black stallion.

She shook herself from the grim thought and frowned.

"No thank you. I actually want to live to see my next birthday," Trixie called after Angela.

Angela stopped, turned, and walked over to the two girls.

"What's that supposed to mean?" she asked, her sunglasses glinting in the light.

"It means that I choose not to ride stallions so that I don't die," Trixie said.

"Why would you die from riding a stallion?"

"Because stallions are dangerous," Trixie stated.

"They are only dangerous if you don't know what you're doing."

Felicity Willoughby had known what she was doing. She was the best dressage rider in the entire world. But look where that knowledge and skill had gotten her.

With Kaela standing right behind her though, Trixie could hardly speak of Felicity's death with such nonchalance. She would have to take the subject in a completely different direction.

"Well unfortunately I am not as talented on horseback as

you are. I'll stick to geldings and mares so that maybe one day I'll be alive to make it to your level," Trixie said.

Angela looked around; Trixie thought that she looked like she had been expecting this altercation.

"But … you are good enough," Angela said softly.

"I think I'll be the judge of that," Trixie said.

And apparently, there was no 'good enough' anyway … The world's greatest dressage rider had met her doom in the saddle of a stallion. Why would Trixie or Angela or any of the rest of them, for that matter, be any different?

ঞ Five ও

Kaela threw the book aside. It was the third horse book she had read and she still had no answers. She wanted a foolproof way to teach the Fairies how to canter without playing follow the leader, but none of the experts wanted to spill the beans.

"Maybe I should write a book," she said, "…one day." She pointed at the bookshelf, "One day, I shall be a published writer and then you will all quake in your writers' circles because I will steal all your readers."

Granted, those books were all non-fiction and she planned to write fiction … But still, quake writers, quake.

She swung her legs off the bed, stood up and stretched. She walked in bare feet across the carpeted floor to her bookshelf and searched the titles. Aside from fiction, there were only horse training books. She needed people training. She could not rely on the experts any more.

"Not that I could rely on them to begin with," Kaela said to herself.

She turned back to stare at her room. Like Kaela herself, her bedroom was loud. It welcomed guests in exclamation marks. Every free inch of wall and ceiling space was taken up by posters of her favourite band, Jamiroquai. She had run out of wall space at the age of twelve and now the band overlapped themselves in a never-ending river of their own faces. Sometimes at night she woke with the moon shining through her windows and balcony patio door, and onto the faces of the band members. She would never admit to anyone that on at least two occasions she had gotten such a fright that she had raced from the room. On one particularly windy and lightning-filled night, the heavy poster that hung directly above her bed had inexplicably peeled itself off the wall and landed face down on top of her. It hadn't helped that the poster was an extreme black and white close-up of the lead singer, and lightning had struck as the poster landed on her face. The room lit up, making the eyes of the man appear more than a little menacing. Her father had not let her live that episode down. Whenever anyone, friend or stranger, mentioned the name Jamiroquai, Leo informed them of the time he had had to rescue his distraught daughter from one of their posters.

That specific poster had been moved to the other side of the room. She now had the band's emblem above the bed: it was safer that way.

She walked to her stereo and turned it on. She needed background music to match the walls before she could concentrate on homework. She then sat down at her desk and took out her English worksheets and notes. She tried to concentrate on Shakespeare but his Old English kept forcing her brain into retreat. No matter how much she tried to concentrate on the questions, she kept losing herself thinking of the stables. Eventually she gave up and went to bed.

First, she made sure the poster was safely stuck to the wall.

It was the land of dreams, or perhaps the world between them, that taught her a way to teach the Fairies what they needed to know – which just proved her father's belief that sleeping cured all of life's problems.

As long as a poster didn't land on top of you that is.

Phoenix: TRIX! Help me!

Trixie: What's up?

Phoenix: What are the names of the planets around the star Bellatrix?

Trixie: They aren't named. They aren't important.

Phoenix: They are important to my play!!!!!!

How can I have a battle for Bellatrix if the planet that houses the aliens isn't named?

Trixie: You're a writer, make up a name.

Trixie knew that writers had no problems in this area. Kaela even struggled to stick to the official titles of things that were named. Not to mention her annoying way of naming inanimate objects. It was all good and well to name a car or a house, but naming your toothbrush 'Papeeto the fifty-sixth' was taking it a bit far.

Phoenix: I can't make something up, I need it as realistic as possible (except, of course, for the insane idea of jump-starting a star with a black hole).

Trixie: Then call it Bellatrix Planet Three.

Phoenix: Why Planet Three?

Trixie: It would have to be the third planet and be in the circumstellar habitable zone, or it wouldn't be able to support water at the three different stages and therefore couldn't support life.

Phoenix: Are you taking into account the size of Bellatrix?

Trixie: I'm sure the habitable planets will be in ratio to the star.

Phoenix: Bellatrix Planet Three!!!!! Perfect!!! I don't have to pay you for that, do I?

Trixie: When I visit Canada, you can take me on a tour as payment.

Phoenix: Snort! I've never been anywhere interesting. I can take you touring on the rez. We have one awesome restaurant called The Big Bear, and that's about it. We have an awesome lake, but it will kill you unless it's summer. Like, really kill you, no exaggeration.

Trixie: Whatever! I've seen the pictures of the mountains surrounding that rez, they are awesome. You can show me those.

Phoenix: Hardly a good payment.

Trixie: You can introduce me to your brothers.

Phoenix: Ewww!!! They are so gross! I don't know what you see in them.

Trixie: GORGEOUS men! Hubba hubba! Is that phrase English?

Phoenix: No one knows what that was. Why don't you just add them on LetsChat?

Trixie: I don't want to look like a crazy stalker.

Phoenix: Of course, telling me to face the laptop to Chiron while he was doing sit-ups doesn't make you a stalker?

Trixie: Of course not: you were the one facing the laptop to him.

Phoenix: You should be a lawyer.

Trixie: I am going to be a scientist with a successful dressage career on the side.

Phoenix: When will you sleep?

Trixie: Sleep is for the weak. Do you ever ride stallions?

Phoenix: We don't believe in gelding our male horses. Why?

Trixie: So you don't see them as dangerous?

Phoenix: Of course not.

This didn't mean a lot coming from a woman who rode in such a way that she would have been banned from Apley five minutes after getting in the saddle (she even rode without a saddle, come to think of it). Phoenix's standards of what was safe riding were in complete contrast to what Trixie had always been taught.

Trixie: Kaela's mom was a world famous rider who used to ride a stallion in competitions. Then one night she fell and died. Or at least, fell and went missing.

Phoenix: That's not the stallion's fault.

Trixie: But she was a brilliant rider. She couldn't possibly have just fallen from a well-behaved horse. *Something* must have happened to her.

Phoenix: *Anything* could have happened. Yesterday I fell off my horse because the sun shone in my eyes when we turned a corner. She was fine, I was blinded. *Anything* can happen on horseback. You can't blame the stallion: if she was a Native rider, the fact that she rode a stallion wouldn't even come into the conversation.

Trixie: I suppose.

Phoenix: What does Kaela think about it?

Trixie: She doesn't talk about it. And we don't bring it up. So don't mention it to her.

Phoenix: My lips are sealed. On a happier note, Satyr is doing push-ups. Want me to take photos?

Trixie hit the video call button and wished she had popcorn.

❧ Six ❧

Kaela made sure she was at the stable long before the first class and that she was the only one to be teaching today. When she had the riders and horses all warmed up, she decided to put her dream to the test.

"Everybody slow down to a walk and listen up," she called.

Shanaeda slowed Star to a walk, Kirsten did the same. The six girls behind them expected the horses to slow down on their own, but the horses expected to be told what to do. It was not a good combination. Caesar nearly ran up Flight's behind, while Apache and Sun Dancer avoided a major collision by forming a V around Caesar who then backed up into an oncoming Rhapsody, who was then bumped into by Jinx. Pumbaa was the only horse to avoid the pile-up – he came to a complete halt quite a distance away because he saw a spot of grass that needed his attention, much to the relief of his mount, Michelle, who was the most junior rider.

"You see what happens when you play follow the leader? Be thankful none of those horses reared or bucked," Kaela said. She knew it was a horrible feeling when instructors rubbed salt in a wound, but she also understood its importance. Eight little faces looked at her from beneath big black hard hats. Kaela had to laugh; they looked like Jack Russell puppies who had been caught digging up the flower beds. It was the look of 'we're sorry – please forgive us, oh and we'll probably do it again later so please forgive us then too.'

Before Kaela could give the command, Shanaeda took the initiative and nudged Star back into a walk, the rest of the girls untangled themselves and fell into formation.

"I am going to try to get you out of the 'follow the leader' habit. You guys are going to try something you have never done before, but we're going to go through it slowly. You ready?" Kaela called.

"Yes," eight little girls answered.

"Okay, what I want you to do is to keep walking. The girl in the front is then going to trot around the ring while the rest of you are still walking. When she catches up with the group, the next girl will trot. You will do this until the first girl is in the front again. When the girl in front of you trots off, keep your horse at a walk. Everybody understand?"

"Yes."

"Good. Everybody ready?"

"Yes."

"Okay then Shanaeda, you're up first," Kaela said.

Shanaeda's grip tightened on the saddle and her little foot nudged Star into a trot. Kirsten held Flight at a walk and led the troops for fifteen seconds of glory. Kaela watched Shanaeda trot around the ring until she reached the back of the group and pulled Star back into a walk. Kaela had to laugh at Star's face: he did not look very impressed with having to walk behind Pumbaa.

"Well done Shanaeda," Kaela smiled, her teaching skills were making her feel rather powerful, "Kirsten, you're up."

Kirsten nudged Flight into a trot and Caesar followed him, but Amy quickly pulled him back to a walk. Kirsten made it all the way back to the group without a hitch.

"Well done Kirsten and Amy. Did everyone see? She pulled him back. If they trot without your permission then pull them back. Okay, who's next?"

One by one the girls trotted around the ring. Kaela had them repeat the exercise several times before she moved on to bigger things.

"Well done girls, that was brilliant. But we're going to try something a bit more difficult." Out of the corner of her eye, Kaela could see Angela come up to the ring and watch. Suddenly she didn't feel so powerful. Kaela took a deep breath to refocus, "Instead of walking, you are going to be trotting and the one in the front will be cantering. Everybody okay with that?"

"Yes," nervous voices answered.

"Well then, trot on."

Shanaeda nudged Star into a trot, Kaela was happy to see that each girl nudged her own horse.

"Whenever you're ready Shanaeda," Kaela had not even finished the sentence before Shanaeda kicked Star into a canter.

She cantered him around the ring, she pulled him back to a trot a little too late, and Star had to dodge Pumbaa to avoid crashing into him.

"Well done Shanaeda, but keep in mind that with a canter you have to start slowing down a lot sooner."

Kirsten and Flight then cantered, Caesar cantered behind him and it took nearly a quarter of the ring for Amy to slow him back to a trot. Eventually he trotted, only to be kicked into a canter mere seconds later. He did not look too happy.

Kaela had the girls go around six more times before she called it quits. By then, the girls had managed to keep the horses in the gait they wanted.

"Well done girls! You should be so proud of yourselves. Give yourselves a round of applause," Kaela was joyous, she did not know whether it was because the girls had succeeded or because her training method had worked. Probably a combination of both. "Well done, now take your horses for an outride and meet me back at the tables when you come back."

Kaela did not have to open the gate for the excited girls,

Angela had done it first. She stood with her foot holding the gate as the girls rode past.

"Well done, you did well," she said to Shanaeda.

"Well done, you looked great," she said to Kirsten.

"Well done," she said to Amy, and then to every girl who passed.

Kaela could not believe what she was hearing; Angela had gone from insulting them to congratulating them. Kaela walked up to her without much hope for a polite conversation.

"Did you see how well they rode every time you said well done?" Angela said as she closed the gate.

"Yes, that's why you say well done. It makes them feel good, so they'll turn around and do it better next time."

Before Angela could answer, Bart called her. She turned to look at him.

"Your mother is waiting for you," he called to her.

Without even turning around, Angela walked off.

"There is something funny about that one," Kaela said, watching the blonde ponytail swing from side to side.

Kaela walked to Quiet Fire's stall, grabbed the package she had safely left there earlier, and went back to the tables. She waited for two minutes before the beginners came running back.

"Well done girls, I don't think you realise what an amazing feat you just conquered."

From the looks on the girls faces – the big smiles, the

dimples, the sparkling eyes – she guessed that statement wasn't exactly true.

"Thank you," eight little voices said shyly.

Kaela reached into her paper bag and pulled out a chocolate bar, she gave it to Jane, "There we go."

"Thank you," Jane said, her smile broadening.

She reached in and brought out seven more and gave them out.

"Well done girls, I'll see you tomorrow."

Kaela walked away happier than the Fairies – she loved helping the little people.

It made her powerful.

"Okay, let's try something we have never done before. Both of you go to the other end of the ring."

Bella and Trixie turned their horses around and walked them to the fence. Out of the corner of her eye, Trixie could see Kaela and Quiet Fire dominating the other ring. Without Bella, there was no one to beat her at jumping.

Except maybe Russell – but Trixie refused to acknowledge him.

Once Bella and Trixie, who interestingly had not said one word to each other in nearly an hour, were stood at the fence facing Wendy, she gave the instruction to drop their reins.

Trixie did so with apprehension.

"All dressage riders need to be able to control their horses without their aids being seen. Meaning, your legs are going to do most of your communicating. We'll start off simple. If you can't do these easy steps, I will send you back to the beginners' class and Kaela can teach you." Wendy teased.

"No way!" Kaela called from the other ring.

"All you have to do, without the use of your reins, is get your horse to walk."

Bella sneered and did it.

Trixie relaxed her body, sat deeply into her saddle and squeezed her calves ever so lightly. Slow-Moe walked forward.

"Now stop."

What? Trixie thought, *How in the name of Epona do you stop without your reins?*

Bella was nearly at the fence on the other side of the ring before she managed it.

Trixie lifted out of her seat without putting pressure with her calves. That didn't work. She sat deeper in the saddle but that just made Slow-Moe walk faster.

Suddenly an image of Felicity Willoughby floated into her mind, although why, Trixie could not say, as Felicity's hands were firmly grasping the reins. She saw Felicity pull up next to Leo, halt Black Satin and throw herself off. She was in her side saddle which meant she had very little contact with the horse when it came to her legs. Everything was in the hands and the weight positioning.

71

And suddenly Trixie had it.

She leaned backwards.

Slow-Moe came to a complete stop.

"Well done, girls. Grab your reins and go back to the other side."

They did as they were told but both girls had visibly paled, they knew what came next.

"Okay, same deal. No reins, only this time, I want you to go straight into a trot and stop before you reach the other side."

Bella dropped her reins and trotted off. But she couldn't stop KaPoe before the fence and nearly fell when he came to a screeching halt.

Trixie's heart palpitated and she had to resist the urge to grab the pommel and hold on. She took a deep breath, rose out of the saddle slightly and squeezed a smidgen harder than she had the first time. Slow-Moe started trotting and Trixie quickly posted for three beats before sitting deeply and leaning back: he half-halted. She quickly moved forward and back again and he came to a full stop.

"Almost. Wanna try again?"

Both girls agreed, but with very little enthusiasm.

Bella managed it quicker the next time. Trixie tried to bring up an image of Felicity again but nothing came. She was on her own.

She took an extremely deep breath, lifted and squeezed. Slow-Moe trotted, she posted for three beats, sat for two and leaned back. He came to a full halt. This time he understood her better.

She smiled and gave him a pat.

And then her breath caught in her throat, she knew what came next.

"Back to the fence," Wendy said and pointed.

The girls nervously took their horses where they rather didn't want them.

"And canter."

Bella, as always, was the first to do it, although she nudged KaPoe too hard and he sprang forward, unsettling her. In order to stop before he jumped the four foot fence, she had no choice but to grab the reins.

"Slow and steady Bella, slow and steady," Wendy informed her with a smile of encouragement.

Felicity was back in Trixie's head. She had always taken almost twice as long to do any dressage routine, but scored nearly double the points. Surely there was a secret buried in there.

Once again, Trixie breathed deeply. She sat as firmly as she could, putting as much weight into her seat as was possible, leaned forward and squeezed Slow-Moe as hard as she could. He pushed himself forward with his back legs and went into a slow canter. Trixie quickly loosened her grip and leaned back, still pushing as much weight into her seat as possible. He came to a complete halt right next to Wendy.

Trixie looked down in breathless excitement.

In the sunlight it was not Wendy who smiled up at her, but Felicity Willoughby in her beautiful blue Victorian riding habit.

Phoenix: A chocolate bar? Your father must have freaked.

Kaela: No, he isn't some kind of food-dictator. Most of his patients eat terribly. So he wouldn't have minded me giving the Fairies chocolate. Not to mention, I didn't tell him. But that's mainly because I used the grocery money to buy them.

Phoenix: Hahahaha!!!! Thank you for brightening up my day. I needed it.

Kaela: Battling Bellatrix giving you trouble?

Phoenix: I would prefer that over what happened today.

Kaela: What happened?

Phoenix: Okay, you have to promise not to laugh. There is a community theatre in the town next to ours. And they are searching for 'local talent' to write their next production. I submitted my play.

Kaela: Why would I laugh at that? Congrats! You must be so proud.

Phoenix: Hardly. I got the letter today telling me that it was not what they were looking for.

Kaela's heart fell into her pelvis, "Ouch!"
Rejection was terrible at the best of times. But when it was your first, it was a million times worse.

Phoenix: I just want to cry.

Kaela: Then cry. Put sad music on and cry until you feel better.

She stopped and tried to think of what her father would say. He was always full of wise words.

Kaela: But remember that failure is part of success. How will you know to do better until you've been told that what you have isn't good enough?

Phoenix: They didn't tell me what was wrong with it though. And I don't have the heart to fix it.

Again. I've fixed it so many times. All I ever do is fix it. I feel like I'm digging a canyon with a tooth-pick.

Kaela: So then don't fix it. Move on to something else. Put it away and come back to it next year when the community theatre is asking for their next production. Next year you will be older and wiser, and will have learnt more. I think we are in desperate need of a Lost Kodas meeting.

Phoenix: For what?

Kaela: To remind you that failure is a step to success. And maybe to give you ideas about your next play.

Phoenix: Why was I talented at something so difficult to actually do? Why do I want to be something that is not unlike walking blindfolded and barefoot in a haunted forest, wondering if your next turn is going to send you over a cliff, or deliver you safely into Dracula's castle where you are finger food for the Count? Why am I talented at the one area of life that is like being surrounded by spirit-eating zombies who want to take your hard work and throw it to the werewolves waiting in the darkness?

Kaela raised her eyebrows.

Kaela: Maybe your next play should be a horror.

⤳ Seven ⤲

Like Trixie herself, her bedroom was simple but cosmic, with a touch of bite. No posters graced the walls, but she had begged and bribed her sister, Melody, to paint the Milky Way across her walls. Her sister had done a brilliant job, the painting looked even better than the photo of the real thing. Of course, once Melody was done, Trixie had taken a red felt tip pen, drawn an arrow to the area earth resided in and wrote, YOU ARE HERE!

The mural may have been Melody, but the humour was all Trixie.

She collapsed on her neatly made double bed and just lay there. She was absolutely exhausted. She remembered the days when Fridays meant sleepovers with Kaela, now they just meant sleep.

She'd had no idea dressage would be this exhausting.

Well, that and riding two horses in one day.

That reminded her, she'd forgotten to bring her backpack home. It was still sitting outside Liquorice's stall.

She sat up quickly and almost sobbed. She would have to cycle the six miles back to get it in the morning.

Just as she almost broke down in tears, she saw her father's car pull up to the gate. She raced out before he could get inside.

"Dad!" she screamed.

"What?" he cried in alarm, "What is it, what's wrong?"

"I left my school bag at the stable."

"What was it doing there anyway? Isn't the rule that you come home first to get changed and then go to the stable?"

"Yes, but this week Liquorice needs someone to ride him so I've been going straight from school."

"And taking your school uniform to the stable and possibly damaging it?"

"It's in my backpack. It's safe."

"So that means you have been taking your expensive horse riding clothes to school squashed in your backpack?"

Trixie nodded slowly. When her father rattled these petty crimes, they somehow didn't seem so petty.

"Hop in, I'll take you. But this ends now. Someone else can ride that horse. You are to stick to the rules we have set down."

Trixie got into the front seat with a heavy heart.

Neither spoke on the ten minute drive to the stable. The only sound in the car was the music from the radio. It was

Kaela's favourite band whose name Trixie, despite ten years of Kaela's near hysteric obsession, could still not pronounce.

Her father, forgetting the dangers the car park possessed, pulled right in and parked as close to the stable as possible. Trixie took that as a bad sign. She hoped she wouldn't have to search for her backpack. Her father's temper seemed to be climbing like a faulty boiler.

She quickly jumped out and raced through the stable. Her backpack wasn't in front of Liquorice's stall, she turned and ran to the tack room where the 'Lost and Found' box sat. Her backpack sat lonely in the box, the soul ruler of a forgotten kingdom. She grabbed it in relief and left the tack room. Her eyes fell on Angela. It was the first time she had seen her on horseback since the day she incurred the eternal wrath of the kodas.

The sight was intoxicating.

She sat confidently in her saddle and put the horse through a dressage routine that Felicity Willoughby would have been at home with. There was a magic between horse and rider. They were one person; like a two-headed centaur. Trixie only dreamed of achieving that level of excellence.

Without knowing why she was doing it, she backtracked back into the tack room and looked at the lists of all the riders. Angela wasn't under advanced rider, nor private owners. It was almost like she didn't belong to the stable. Just as she was about to turn away, Trixie saw the name *Angela May* on another list entirely.

"Private tutelage. What does that mean?"

She was the only one on the list.

But that didn't matter to Trixie, she had what she was after: Angela's full name.

She raced back to the car where she hopped in just in time to hear the DJ say, "Jamiroquai!"

"That's Kaela's favourite band," she said to her father, "Their poster tried to kill her once."

"Leo can't finish that story without landing up on the floor in a heap. One day he is going to have an aneurysm from all the laughing."

Trixie chuckled, glad that something had dispersed her father's rage.

The two-headed centaur came into the car park then, on their way to an outride. While her father waited for them to pass before reversing, Trixie took a good look at Angela May.

How much did she know about dressage?

Did she have all the secrets?

Secrets Trixie would have been able to get from Felicity if fate had not intervened?

Was Angela May a keeper of knowledge?

On Saturday morning, Kaela sprung out of bed as the sun sprang out of the horizon. She had no idea what time Angela had class, or if she even had class on a Saturday. But she planned to get to the stables as soon as possible just in case. She wanted to see Sunglasses Girl ride. She threw on her riding clothes without bothering to look in the mirror, only noticing that her chaps were on wrong when her legs kept getting caught on each other. She was sitting in the bathroom on the edge of the tub redoing them when Alice walked in.

"I thought we were going shopping for new chaps today," Alice said, picking up her toothbrush.

"We can still go, I just have a few things to do at the stable. I'll be back at about twelve," Kaela said as she did the last buckle.

"Don't worry about walking back, I'll come fetch you. We can go straight from the stable."

"Great stuff."

"Great stuff," Alice said through a mouthful of toothpaste.

She left her grandmother, bolted into the kitchen, grabbed an apple and escaped through the back door before the dogs woke up. She ate her apple on the short walk to the stable, noticing how the crash of the nearby ocean echoed across the flat lands surrounding them. A cargo ship from China sat bobbing in the harbour. Some riders from rival schools rode past, gossiping about some boy at their stable. Derrick rode bareback while pulling Jeremy along behind him.

"The fool chased a car down the road. Took me twenty minutes to find him," he said with an aggravated shake of his head.

"That donkey is more trouble than he is worth," Kaela called back, but Derrick was already through the gates.

As Kaela walked into the car park, white graffiti caught her eye. She walked over to it. Scrawled across the notice board in white chalk were the words:

IMPORTANT MEETING FOR <u>ALL</u> RIDERS.
MONDAY AFTER THE BEGINNERS' CLASS.
SPREAD THE WORD!

"Interesting. Very, very interesting," Kaela said in her best *Sherlock Holmes* impersonation. She turned on her heel and walked towards the ring.

To her surprise and amazement, her eyes fell on Angela sitting proudly in her saddle. She rode the chestnut Thoroughbred who now existed in a stall bearing the plaque, 'Fergie'.

Fergie seemed to be enjoying the dressage routine she was being put through. Her ears perked forward excitedly and her big eyes sparkled. Kaela looked down at her watch (which had just received a new battery), it had just gone seven o'clock, yet here was Angela on horseback. Most of the horses in the stable had not even had their breakfast yet, never mind been tacked, warmed up and put through a complicated dressage routine.

"That's determination," for both horse and rider."

Kaela got bored of watching the same routine, she had

never had any patience for dressage – she believed it took the excitement out of riding. What was the point of making the horse do monkey tricks when you could ride the back of the wind or fly through the air?

She made her way to Quiet Fire's stall; the horse was still asleep and had no intention of waking up any time before breakfast. Kaela had never been to the stable this early and could not believe the difference the hour made. There were no usual stable sounds or sights, it even smelled slightly different.

"Interesting. Very, very interesting." Sherlock Holmes said.

She walked to the tack room, found the dirtiest tack around, grabbed it and the cleaning equipment, and made her way to the tables.

Once she had gotten comfortable and began working on Liquorice's bridle, she noticed something she had failed to see before. It was not Wendy nor Derrick or Bart who taught Angela, it was a man she had never seen before. Kaela watched with concentration as the three in the ring performed an accomplishment she had only ever seen one other rider do.

And she refused to think of that particular rider or what she was capable of.

The trainer stood on one side of the ring while Angela and Fergie stood on the other. When the trainer lifted his right arm, Fergie stepped forward with her left leg. When the trainer lifted his left arm, Fergie stepped forward with her right leg. Because the two stood facing each other, their lefts and rights were on different sides, therefore Fergie's leading leg always matched the upheld arm. Kaela knew that it was Angela commanding the horse, but she could not see the rider giving any commands and Kaela herself had no idea how you would get a horse to do that. It looked as though it was being done by magic.

Angela deserves a chocolate, Kaela thought in wonder.

Once Fergie had reached the trainer, he put both hands down. Kaela had expected the instructor's usual cries of congratulations, followed by a loving pat on the obedient horse's neck. But this trainer gave none of these.

"Go back to the other end and do it again, but this time on the opposite side," was all he said.

Kaela was in shock, she had never heard of a trainer who did not congratulate a rider on a task well done. It was simply not heard of. Her eyes quickly swept to Angela's face: for a second she thought she saw disappointment, then Angela returned to her normal hard-set concentration.

If Kaela had been riding, she would have simply walked the horse to the other end of the ring, but Angela was apparently too impatient for that slow gait. Kaela witnessed something she thought she would only see in movies. Angela gently kicked Fergie and turned her at the same time, the horse's front legs lifted slightly off the ground and her back legs turned her 180 degrees and pushed her forward into a canter. When they reached the other side, the action was repeated, although instead of bolting forward, Fergie stood in a perfect upright position. The duo looked like they were made of wax. Kaela had just seen her second bout of magic for the day. She imagined that this must be what it was like for people who could not ride and managed to witness the horse riding portion of the Empire Games. It must appear as though the riders are controlling the horse by some supernatural phenomenon.

If Kaela had thought the earlier dressage display was beautiful, she could not have found words to describe what she saw next (which was probably a bad thing considering her writing aspirations). When the trainer lifted his right arm, Fergie stepped forward with her right leg, when the left arm lifted, the left leg stepped forward. It looked as though there was an imaginary cross between trainer and horse. When Fergie stood before him, he sent the pair back to the other side without a word of praise to be heard.

How does Angela know if she is doing anything right if she never gets told? Kaela thought.

She did not agree with this man's teaching methods, even if she was only an amateur teacher herself.

Next Angela and Fergie had to do something Kaela had almost forgotten existed. The trainer lifted both hands into the air, he then crossed his left arm over his right arm – Fergie crossed her right leg over her left leg. When he crossed his right arm over his left, Fergie crossed her left leg over her right.

"Let's do it the opposite way," he called.

When he crossed his right arm, she crossed her right leg.

Kaela knew that move very well. She couldn't do it. Nor did she know how to do it. But that move, called 'Felicity's Cross', had been invented and presented to the judges at the Empire Games nearly twenty years ago by her own mother. Her mother had worn her world famous Victorian riding habit even though she had not been in a side saddle. From that, Kaela could guess her mother had needed her legs for the aids.

'Felicity's Cross' was not done at Apley, or any other riding school Kaela knew of. It was too complicated, horses had to be too trained and, even if anyone could do it, no one did it in front of Kaela.

There was an unwritten rule that dressage champion and Empire Games gold medallist Felicity Willoughby, was not mentioned in front of Kaela.

She didn't mind, she liked it that way.

Angela either did not know who Kaela's mother was, or didn't care. Strangely, either way, it felt quite heart-warming to see somebody do it.

She had been holding her breath during the forbidden move, and it was only when her lungs began aching that she let herself breathe. She let out a loud sigh that caught Fergie's attention. The chestnut looked over; Kaela smiled at her, forgetting that the horse couldn't smile back.

"That's our lesson; take the horse for an outride. I'll see

you in the ring at eight," the trainer called, and opened the gate for her. There was not so much as a 'well done' from him as she passed.

"Barbarian," Kaela said under her breath.

If Kaela had been a braver person she would have congratulated Angela herself. But the mahogany-haired girl could not bring herself to speak to the person who had been so mean to her. She was also rather too tongue-tied after witnessing 'Felicity's Cross' for the first time in almost ten years.

Angela passed without a word.

Because Kaela had been so wrapped up in the magic (and heartache) of Angela's lesson, she had failed to see that Apley Towers had sprung to life around her. The grooms were walking about carrying feeding buckets and small hay bales, horses stuck their heads out of stalls expectantly, and private owners were arriving – most of them old enough to drive here. Huge groups of older teenage girls gathered in the parking lot discussing boyfriends, overbearing parents, and whatever else it was that eighteen- and nineteen-year-olds discussed.

Kaela dreaded reaching that age: not only were you expected to drive yourself around, but conversations were as monotonous as a fast food menu. Had she ever actually heard that group of women discussing anything but men and make-up and hair? How unbelievably unfulfilled their lives must be. Even Alice's conversations on baking were more interesting than theirs (although Kaela had to admit, Alice threw the odd Pagan ritual into her conversations: those witches did tend to spice things up a bit).

She was so absorbed in cleaning Liquorice's saddle that she did not notice the two boys standing next to her. When one of them touched her shoulder, her soul jumped right out of her mouth, screamed blue murder and jumped right back in.

"Sorry, I didn't mean to scare you," the boy said.

Kaela recognised him at once; it was Bart's best friend, Björn. She was surprised to see him out and about, he never graced the sunlight with his presence – his computer games were far too important.

"Do you mind if we sit?" Bart asked from behind her.

Kaela shook her head and the boys took a seat on each side of her.

"So, how are you?" Björn asked, rather awkwardly.

"I'm fine, why aren't you with your electronic wife?" Kaela asked.

"I'm taking a break, she's tired," Björn said.

"He's lying," Bart jumped in, "His computer bombed out this morning and I'm not even sure we can get it back on."

"So you decided to come ride instead?" Kaela asked in her most sickly-sweet voice.

"HA! You will never get me on one of those overgrown fleabags," Björn said with fake certainty, there was a slight look of worry in his eyes.

"Well, Liquorice does need some exercise or else he might start cribbing, which could be dangerous," Bart teased.

"Yes, if he starts cribbing he'll chew on his stable door and he might just swallow a bit of wood, and then he could get colic," Kaela joined.

"And if he gets colic then he could die," Bart added.

"You wouldn't want to be responsible for an innocent horse's death, would you?" Kaela said with big, sad eyes.

"That's not going to work on me," Björn said, but there was a hint of worry in his voice. Before the conversation could go any further, Angela led her other horse, Dawn, into the ring. The three watched her check the stirrups, mount and begin walking. Kaela then remembered the trainer.

"Who trains her?" she asked Bart.

"Her own personal trainer, I don't know his name. He comes in every morning, trains her, then leaves for his next rich client I suppose," Bart said, not taking his eyes off the horse and mount.

"So why is she at this stable if she is being taught by somebody else?"

"Because he doesn't have his own stable and she had to keep her horses somewhere," Bart looked at her, his deep blue eyes twinkling, "Are you doubting the superiority of our stable?"

"No," she said sweetly, "Just curious about the new arrangement."

"Curiosity killed the cat."

"But satisfaction brought it back it again."

"You still owe me chocolate."

Kaela looked at his dimple, at the corner of his smile, and at the twinkle in his bright blue eyes.

Suddenly Björn broke the silence, "He wouldn't really get colic would he?" he asked in a shaking voice.

Bart and Kaela laughed until Jeremy came over to inspect the ruckus and pushed Björn off his chair. Then they laughed harder.

Half an hour later the three were on horseback in the feeding paddock – Kaela atop Quiet Fire, Bart on his own horse, Mouse, and Björn on Liquorice. The beautiful Arabian seemed to understand that he had an amateur on his back and he did everything with special care.

Kaela led the three person parade, while Bart rode next to Björn in case of danger. The three kept at a walk while Björn got used to his mount; this left Kaela's mind to wander. And it wandered straight to Angela. Despite the fact that Angela was an amazing rider, she didn't get congratulated. It had probably been like that for so long that she was used to it.

Well, when Trixie told her she was a good rider she actually got defensive, Kaela thought.

That was why Angela was so fascinated with the positive effect saying 'well done' had had on the Fairies. Then, maybe she had not personally meant to insult the Fairies, maybe it had not made sense to her that their faults could be explained to them at a better time. Angela had made no faults today but Kaela was willing to bet her new chaps that when Angela did make a fault, she heard about it. In Angela's mind, she had not been insulting the beginners, she had been teaching them the way she had been taught. And when Kaela confronted her she had become defensive, the same way that Kaela herself had gotten defensive. Kaela had seen the real Angela when they had spoken after she had jumped Quiet Fire.

"Just keep your heels down."

Behind her, Bart continued with his lesson.

Kaela wasn't sure what she should do with this new-found information: did it really make a difference in her life? Her head was quick to answer NO! But her heart kept saying something else. Her heart was convinced that this information made a very big difference in her life.

"Earth to Kaela! Hello! Space Cowgirl, hello!"

Kaela spun around, she had been in such a daze that she had not even heard them talking to her.

"What?"

"Björn thinks he's ready to trot," Bart said.

"Really?" she hadn't been ready to trot in her first lesson.

"Just keep it at a slow trot," Björn added.

Kaela tightened her grip and nudged Quiet Fire into a trot; she held the reins tight to prevent him from going any faster. She wasn't used to going this slow; she was finding it difficult to get in the motion. As she usually went faster, she didn't keep her seat out of the saddle long enough and kept going down when the horse was still going up. She had to keep double bouncing to get back into the proper motion. She couldn't help but laugh at herself: she was very out of practice when it came to the basics.

I'm so focused on the more difficult things that I've forgotten how to do the easy ones, Kaela thought.

Life was funny sometimes.

"Having a bit of trouble are we?" Bart asked from behind her.

"Just waiting for my bum to catch up with the rest of my body," she called back.

Kaela tried a different approach: she went into a sitting trot, felt the difference in time between Quiet Fire going up and Quiet Fire going down, and adapted herself to it.

"There!" she cried when she had succeeded.

"Your bum catch up?" Björn called.

"Yes."

How strange that achieving something so simple in the saddle made her feel so powerful?

Maybe that was the secret to riding … Be good at the simple things and the rest will take care of itself.

The three rode as they were until Björn felt confident enough to go a bit faster. Kaela loosened her grip on the reins, squeezed a little harder with her calf muscles, and fell into Quiet Fire's quicker motion.

Soon Björn was confident enough to go all out, "How do you get this fleabag to gallop?" he asked.

"You want to gallop?" Bart asked and raised one eyebrow.

"I challenge you!" Björn declared.

Before either of them could say a word, Kaela turned Quiet Fire around and kicked him into a gallop. The other horses played follow the leader and the riders did nothing to stop them.

It was an exciting race: all three horses were nose to nose. Because of his sheer size, Mouse began gaining ground. Soon he was a whole head in front of the other two, then a neck. Just as his shoulder was about to pass Quiet Fire's nose, the gelding put in another effort and shot in front of Mouse. Kaela looked behind her, the look of surprise on Bart's face made her feel more powerful than she already did. Despite his surprise, he was catching up fast. The two horses, once again, ran nose to nose. Liquorice, not to be outdone, put in a last effort. It's always been said that the speed of a horse is not in his feet but in his heart, and Liquorice proved this as he raced past Quiet Fire and Mouse, leaving them both to wonder what had just happened. Liquorice won the race by a full horse's length, even though he had a rider that had to hang on for dear life.

Kaela laughed long and hard into Quiet Fire's mane. An amateur had just beaten both an intermediate and advanced rider. Mouse seemed to take it the hardest, his ears were flat against his head and his lower lip sulked.

"I don't think he's too happy to get beaten by a show horse," Bart said.

Poor Mouse, Kaela thought, *he is a bit of a sore loser.*

Kaela turned to look at the riding rings, Wendy and Derrick were building jumps in the advanced ring. She looked at her watch: it was almost time for the adult classes. Kaela could also see Angela grooming Dawn; the small horse looked as though she was in heaven.

The three took their horses for an outride, brought them back to the stable and dismounted. Wendy was already teaching the adult's class, Kaela knew somebody would be looking for Quiet Fire soon so she took him to his stall, loosened his girth and tied his reins in a loose knot. She gave him a farewell hug and kiss on the nose and walked back to the riding ring. Surprisingly enough, Alice sat at the table talking to Derrick, despite the fact that it wasn't even eleven o'clock yet. The wind brought parts of their conversation to Kaela's ears.

"… riding long enough," Derrick said.

"… is ready … So frustrating … Felicity would have known," Alice said.

Kaela had no idea what they were talking about, but it really didn't interest her, particularly after they mentioned her mother's name.

"Hi Grandma," Kaela said as she came up to the table.

"Hi sweetheart," Alice said and put her arm around Kaela's waist.

"What do you think of our new rider?" Derrick asked pointing to Angela.

Before Kaela could remember that she was not particularly fond of Angela, the image of the blonde rider on Fergie that morning crept into her mind.

"She is amazing, have you seen her doing dressage?" Kaela asked.

Before Derrick could answer, Alice interrupted.

"New rider?"

"Angela May. She's just moved to the stable. They live one town over. Her mother teaches at the university. She has caused something of a stir around here as she is only fifteen, but rides better than I do." Derrick folded his arms.

Kaela's eyes fell on her grandmother's open handbag; her own mobile caught her attention. One missed call. She grabbed it. Trixie had called an hour ago and left a voice message. Kaela walked away to listen to it.

"Hello Kae, you gone shopping for chaps yet? What else you getting up to today? Got a family thing happening at my grandmother's house later today. I just phoned to tell you that there is a meeting for all riders on Monday after the first class. Russell phoned to tell me. Pass it on to everybody you know. Okay, enjoy your day, wish me luck for mine," Trixie kissed the phone twice before putting it down.

Kaela laughed at her friend – she could not escape Russell no matter how hard she tried.

"Ready to go?" Alice asked, as she came up behind her.

"Yup."

"Come on then, Space Cowgirl."

Trixie looked at the list of Angela Mays on LetsChat. There were a lot of them. Some hadn't bothered to put profile pictures up, so she couldn't tell if they were the one she was looking for. Who bothers to have a LetsChat account with no picture? What was the point of it then?

A scented breeze came in through the window. Trixie looked away from the computer and out into the garden. Her grandmother spent eighteen hours a day tending to the flowers. Trixie hadn't quite worked out why. Flowers couldn't feed you and generally speaking they fed themselves, so why tend them? Yes, they fed butterflies and bees, but then nature would have tended them. What was the point of making your garden look cultivated when nature would have done a better job no matter what?

The feeding paddock at Apley Towers was left to grow wild as it meant more nutrition for the horses. This also led to an almost mind-boggling amount of wildlife. It was the only place in Port St. Christopher where entire colonies of meerkats and bushbabies lived, where kites and eagles routinely circled looking for elephant shrews, who dodged them by hiding in the full brush. Rabbits, geese, ducks, guinea fowl, monkeys and unending amounts of insect species lived quite amicably within the meadows.

There was nothing like that in her grandmother's more 'sophisticated' garden. It was plain and arduous on the eyes in its barrenness. Maybe Trixie should suggest a goat, it would save her grandmother having to weed and at least she would get milk out of it.

Who knows, maybe the goat would liven the place up a little.

She turned back to the computer and decided to search Angela Mays in South Africa only. Three came up. The last one had posted a status in La Lucia yesterday. Trixie smiled and clicked the profile picture. La Lucia was one town over from Port St. Christopher. In fact, Trixie was there at that moment.

The profile picture was of a badge of the South African flag with a gold feather wrapped around it. A Springbok and Blue Crane – the country's national animal and bird – each held an end of the feather. Trixie knew this badge, although she had never seen it in real life. It was the badge given to those who had earned their South African colours in any sport. In other words, Angela had competed and represented South Africa in an international competition. No easy feat.

Trixie went through Angela's account, all the while feeling like a would-be bank robber watching the security footage to find the weak points.

Angela seemed to go through spurts where dressage was her favourite and then back to jumping. Articles she had shared and statuses she had put up fluctuated between the two. It appeared she was at the top of a dressage wave at the moment. Every status for the last few weeks was about Fergie and their routines. It came as no surprise to see that Angela had been watching video clips of Felicity Willoughby. Her side saddle Empire Games win had been put on Angela's profile only the day before. Trixie clicked on the comments and read as Angela and some other woman with a horse profile picture discussed the merits and flaws of learning to ride in such a useless saddle. From what Angela commented, Trixie could guess that she was in fact a keeper of dressage knowledge, just as she suspected. So advanced and full of dressage jargon was this conversation that Trixie couldn't follow it. The last comment, though, severely stuck out.

Felicity Willoughby used to live in Port St. Christopher. I think her family is still there. I wonder if her daughter rides? The horse profile picture woman had said.

Angela had not answered.

"I wonder if you know who Kaela is."

She doubted it. Angela wouldn't have come across Kaela's surname. Besides, there were quite a few Willoughbys living in and near the town. Leo had two brothers who each had four children. There would be no way to pinpoint Kaela as Felicity's daughter if you were going by surname alone. And even if Angela knew of Kae's illustrious mother, wouldn't that mean that as a fan of Felicity, Angela would be thrilled to know Kaela?

Unless she was jealous. If she was simply jealous, as everyone assumed Bella was, then the rules changed. Then she became just another Bella.

Trixie found herself caught in a complex vortex: Angela had made an instant enemy of Kae and therefore should be an enemy of Trixie. But Angela had knowledge and skills that Trixie desperately wanted – especially now that her classes were with Bella. How much would Kaela hate her if she asked Angela a simple question?

Too much, Trixie eventually decided, and went back to the barbecue and the goatless, cultivated land.

⚜ Eight ⚜

After a quick lunch of veggie delight sandwiches, Kaela and Alice walked into Pennylane – it was the biggest tack shop in Port St. Christopher, and the only place Kaela would ever go for tack and riding gear. She knew the store backwards and could walk to the chaps with her eyes closed. The shop was divided into three rooms – one for saddles, bridles, reins and bits; another for everything else the horse would need, and the last for the rider. The saddle room was directly opposite the rider room with the doors facing each other. Kaela walked through to the chaps while Alice hung back to talk to Sandy, the owner. Kaela was sorry to lose her chaps, she liked them: they were one of a kind and she hadn't found any like them since. As opposed to zips, they had Velcro and buckles. Kaela believed that was why they had lasted so long. Trixie and Russell, as well as other riders from the intermediate class, constantly broke the zips on their chaps and had to have them replaced. Kaela would miss her chaps that never broke. She found a pair she thought would fit and sat down on the ground to try them on.

"Mom, you are being completely unreasonable."

Kaela looked up. That was Angela's voice. It was coming from the saddle room.

"I am not being unreasonable, your saddle is broken, you need a new one."

"My saddle is not broken, it's just a little scuffed. It's not going to impair my riding."

"It's not about whether or not it impairs your riding, it's about looking good – you have competitions to win."

"I'll win a competition based on my riding skill, not the look of my saddle."

"Angela, I am surprised at you. The way you are behaving, you would think that I was making you pay for the saddle. Honestly, most girls would love to get a brand new saddle. Why are you putting up such a fight?"

"I don't see the point of buying a new saddle for no reason. I then have to ride this new saddle in until it is comfortable. And for what? Nothing."

"It is not nothing. The other one looks like it has been dragged backwards through a bush by a thylacoleo."

Kaela's eyebrows rose in surprise. A thylacoleo was a prehistoric marsupial from Australia. It had been extinct for over forty-five thousand years. Kaela honestly believed she was the only person in the whole of Port St. Christopher who knew that at one point in Australian history there was a carnivorous marsupial that may have hunted humans and was closely related to the Koala bear (which, thankfully, doesn't hunt humans).

"It is well-used," Angela said.

"You are also being judged by how well turned out you are. Would you take a well-used saddle to the Empire Games?"

"If it won me gold, then yes."

The two began moving further away; Kaela crept closer to the door. She peeped around to see Angela's mother rub her hand up and down a black saddle.

"What about this one?"

Angela turned to look at her mother.

"That saddle is too big for Dawn."

"How would you know?"

"I ride the horse, Mother; I know what type of saddle she needs."

"Why are you so crabby today? Did you get into a fight with someone at the stables?"

"No, this is not like the other stable: nobody fights at this stable."

Kaela bit her cheeks to hold back a laugh; Angela had clearly not met Bella just yet.

"How can nobody fight? It's a competitive atmosphere – people in competition always fight."

"But it's not competitive, everybody is so nice to each

other, everybody helps each other out, they even tack each other's horses. It's calm and relaxed and everybody can ride whenever they want as long as they do work around the stable. Yesterday, two girls from the intermediate class got to spend half the day riding two school horses free of charge because they had spent the other half of the day cleaning tack and mucking stalls."

"Sounds interesting," Angela's mom said, she didn't sound very interested though.

"It's just so relaxed there Mom, everybody is relaxed and they just enjoy riding."

"Well I don't want you to get relaxed: you have competitions to win. You are not going to win anything by being relaxed."

"You should see the riders, Mom, they ride because they love to ride and they are good because they love to ride. You should see this girl, Trixie, she is so good at dressage but she doesn't have the right horse to win, and that doesn't matter to her, because even if she doesn't win she is still getting to do what she loves."

"Well it matters to you whether or not you are going to win, and you still do what you love. Now your father and I have made a lot of sacrifices to get you where you are. The life that you insist you want is very expensive. The least you could do is cooperate."

Kaela ducked behind the wall as Angela's mother turned around and walked towards the door.

"Now this discussion is over. Being relaxed and calm is not going to get you anywhere; working hard on the horse is going to make you a winner. We'll buy another saddle closer to the competition."

Kaela shrunk further backwards as Angela's mother walked out the door.

"Are there at least any cute boys at this stable?" she asked.

Angela shrugged.

"Who is the blue-eyed wonder that came to the car the other day?"

"Bart Oberon. Wendy's son."

"Hmm ... Angela Oberon."

Fire erupted across Kaela's brain.

"Mom, you are so embarrassing!" Angela cried and backtracked.

"I'm teasing. Relax. You are so tightly wound. After just giving me a whole speech about being relaxed, you're now the one who is coiled like a viper."

"I'm not allowed to be distracted by other riders but I am allowed to be distracted by boys? Mother, you make no sense."

Her mother laughed, "I just know how to get a rise out of you. Tell me about Bart."

"He likes Kaela."

"What are you doing?" a voice asked from inside the room.

Kaela turned to look; she didn't have time to consider what

Angela had just said about Bart. The voice belonged to a boy who must have been about seventeen. He had breeches on as well as riding boots, but no shirt. Kaela looked at his naked stomach; it was a rider's stomach, muscles made strong by hours of posting. She looked behind him; the door leading to a paddock was open, he must have just come through it.

He raised his black eyebrows at her. Kaela looked around: she was crouched beneath the riding jackets, with only one shoe on and half her chap undone – it flapped like a broken wing around her calf. The new chaps were still gripped in her hands, which happened to be dragging on the dirty floor; she ripped them up and began dusting them off.

"I ... was ..."

What was she doing? Eavesdropping on a conversation she should definitely not have heard? Getting the shop's chaps dirty? Staring at a seventeen-year-old's naked stomach? "I was trying on new chaps."

"On the floor?" he asked.

"No other place to sit."

"Why are you underneath the riding jackets?"

Kaela looked up at the hems of an entire row of navy blue riding jackets, "They help me get into the horse spirit."

"I see," he didn't see, he frowned and looked dubious. "Do you need some help?"

"No, I ... I'm good," Kaela said, she cursed herself for blushing.

"Why don't I just help you anyway?" he obviously thought

108

she was a bit mad. He pulled a stool out from underneath the jodhpur shelf and patted the seat.

Kaela walked over and sat down. He held his hands out for the chaps, she dusted them once more before giving them to him. He crouched in front of her and put her foot on his leg. He undid the chap, took it off, and balanced it on his other leg. He then put the new chap on her leg and pulled the zip up. He looked up at her for the first time; he had dull blue eyes, almost as if they were bored.

"How's that feel?"

"A little strange but really nice even though there must be a three year age gap between us," Kaela forgot that he was asking about the chaps.

"How old are you?"

"Fourteen."

"Turning fifteen this year?"

"In August."

"Then yes, there is a three year age gap. But how does the chap feel?"

That was when Kaela realised what she had just said: she blushed redder than a tomato on a hot day.

"I ... ah ... the chap feels good," she said, even though she couldn't feel anything because she was sat down.

He took her leg off his leg and picked up her other one, he repeated the action.

"How does that feel?"

This time, Kaela completely forgot to answer.

"Maybe you should walk around, August, feel if they are comfortable."

Kaela stood up and walked to the door, saw her grandmother, and quickly turned around.

What would Gramoo say if she saw me cavorting with this man? Kaela thought with panic.

She looked back at the shirtless rider, who patted the chair again. She returned to her seat.

On the way back she noticed that the chaps felt great, they weren't loose or tight.

When she had sat down again, he picked up her foot and put it back on his leg, this time he let her heel hang over the edge.

"Pretend your foot is in a stirrup," he said.

Her heel automatically went down.

"How does that feel?"

It felt a lot better than her old chaps did, "Feels good," she breathed rather than said.

"Well then, August, I think we have found your chaps."

"Kaela?"

Kaela looked at the doorway. Angela and her mother stood in the doorway staring at Kaela with her foot on the shirtless rider's leg.

"Well I guess Bart is yours for the taking now," Angela's mother said with a smirk and walked off.

Kaela quickly pulled her foot back and began undoing the zips.

"Anything I can do for you?" the shirtless rider asked Angela.

"I wanted to buy some gloves, but I'm not so sure my mother would approve of how you sell your stock," Angela answered, raising her eyebrows.

"It's a service with a smile."

"Whose? Yours or the customer?"

"The customer of course, it is my job to make them smile. Their pleasure is my concern."

Kaela stripped the chaps off, grabbed both pairs and looked at the boy, "Thanks, they're great, I'll take them," she said, and stood up.

"Thanks for stopping by, August, do come again."

Kaela walked past Angela without looking at her; she had never been so embarrassed in all her life.

Angela looked at the shirtless rider, he looked at her with his bored eyes, then he patted the seat. Angela laughed and went to sit down.

To Kaela's horror, Alice stood talking to Angela's mother at the till.

"No, Kaela does not have her own horse just yet, we are letting her ride as many horses as we can before we buy her one. That is the technique I used for my daughter and it worked perfectly the first time. Although unlike her mother, Kaela seems to stick to riding only one horse."

"Quiet Fire and I are in love," Kaela said, and put the chaps on the counter.

"Are those the ones you want?" Alice asked.

"Yup – they fit great – can't wait to ride in them – wish I was on a horse right now – riding free in the open air – no boys – everybody wearing shirts – is it just me or is it stuffy in here?"

The three adults looked at Kaela questioningly.

Finally Sandy broke the silence, "Will that be all?"

"Yes," Kaela said, a little louder than she needed to.

Her grandmother raised her eyebrows.

"Well Angela has two horses," Gwendolyn May, Angela's mother, said, as though there had not been an interruption. "One for dressage and one for jumping. She is actually competing in a very well-to-do jumping show in two weeks' time. It's very exciting; she has been entering for the last three years and has won in all three years. Does Kaela compete in anything?" she asked pompously.

"She enters when her stable enters, but she doesn't always win. I prefer it that way. Then, when she is grown up and loses in real life, it isn't that much of a shock. The most disastrous thing that could happen to a child is if they win everything and never find out that if they lose, life will still go on," Alice said, equally pompously.

Before the discussion could go any further, Angela walked up to the till wearing black, velvet gloves.

"Are those the ones you've chosen?" her mother asked.

"Yes – best gloves I've ever bought," she turned to face her mother, "This store has the world's best salesman."

"Why, what has he done?"

Kaela and Angela were quiet.

Finally, Kaela – ever the storyteller – said, "He gave us a lesson on quantum mechanics."

That sounded believable. No one understood quantum mechanics, there would be no questions.

Except, Angela shook her head quite violently.

"Since my mom teaches astrophysics at the university, she knows quantum mechanics inside and out," Angela said, looking at Kaela with big eyes, indicating that she had well and truly put her foot in it.

"Oh this isn't real quantum mechanics, this is Hollywood quantum mechanics. Like time travel." Kaela quickly claimed.

"Time travel is possible," Angela's mother said, "Space travel is essentially time travel."

Kaela stared at her in shock.

"Next she is going to tell us that teleportation is possible," Alice said with a chuckle.

Gwendolyn May shrugged and said, "It is a quantum theory that has existed for decades and it is possible using small particles."

"I'll never watch a science-fiction film in the same way again," Kaela said with a slow shake of her head, knitting her eyebrows and thinking she should research her story ideas before blurting them out next time.

"The only thing I know about the cosmos is that outside

of our solar system there's a star called Andromeda," Sandy said.

"Andromeda isn't a star, it is an entire galaxy. In fact, Andromeda is hurtling towards us and our two galaxies will one day collide."

Sandy, Kaela, Alice and the rest of the shoppers stared at Angela's mother in horror.

"Oh don't worry. Our sun will die in a massive explosion, taking out the four closest planets, long before that happens."

"Oh that makes it better," Alice said.

KW: *We are all doomed, people! Doomed! The sun is going to explode and destroy the four closest planets, and Andromeda is rushing towards us and is going to collide with us. We are all doomed.*

Her status had caused quite an uproar from most of her friends. The worried, stupefied and just generally flabbergasted comments made her laugh.

A small blue box popped up in the corner of her screen.

Phoenix: My big big big bro, Chiron, says to tell you that the galaxies colliding won't happen for another 3.75 billion years, so you shouldn't worry about it.

Kaela: What about my descendants?

Phoenix: They will have to deal with it.

Kaela: Poor fools.

Phoenix: Why are you suddenly Miss Science?

Kaela: Ran into Angela at the tack shop. Her mother is an astrophysicist, so she just informed us of our star's impending doom and the collision of two galaxies. Such good information to get on a Saturday afternoon.

Phoenix: Her mother is an astrophysicist? And I thought my A in science was pretty impressive.

Kaela: I thought my knowledge of the solar system was pretty good … I'm not so sure any more. Although, she may be able to tell me all about teleportation of single cells and time travel through black holes, but I bet she could never tell me why Saturn's moon is named Titan. Saturn is the ROMAN God of agriculture and Titan is a GREEK God.

Phoenix: Preach it sister.

Kaela: How can they mix the two?

Phoenix: How dare they?

Kaela: Or are they trying to suggest something?

Phoenix: What are they trying to suggest?

Kaela: By naming a planet after a Roman God and naming a lowly moon after a Greek God, are they suggesting that Roman Gods are better than Greek Gods?

Phoenix: Oh the cheek of it!

Kaela: But then why would they name an entire galaxy after a Greek princess? Are they just trying to confuse us?

Phoenix: Chiron says that they are scientists, not historians.

Kaela: Obviously.

✎ Nine ❧

Monday came far too soon. Weekends always seemed to sail by and before she knew it, Kaela was back at school learning things she rather wouldn't, and having her intelligence tested on the basis of how much information she could regurgitate, and how closely the regurgitation resembled the textbook. Her role as sub-editor of the school's newspaper kept her chasing lazy journalists to get their articles so the newspaper could be printed on Friday – a role she was ready to quit by the end of the day.

"Having any luck?" Tessigan Brailyn, the editor, asked as she dropped her articles off.

"Empty promises."

"What fun."

Kaela took a cursory glance at the articles already collected, "Gossip, gossip, celebrity stalking. Ha! News of the world? Yet it's an article on some prince going on holiday somewhere. How is that news?"

Tess shrugged, "Some people are monarchists."

"Sounds more like a masochist to me."

Tess put both hands in the air, "What are you gonna do?"

Kaela tossed the articles on the desk, "We have a very lame newspaper this month."

Tess took a sip of water from her bright pink bottle and raised her eyebrows.

"You said it."

"What are we gonna do?"

"Well the two of us are going to have to write something."

"Oh great, more articles of *substance*."

That word made Kaela's skin creep: it was the quickest way to make a chore of the beautiful act of writing "What are you going to write on?"

Tess shrugged, "Maybe the present political climate in the Middle East versus the so-called democracies in the west."

"Yes, because fourteen-year-olds want to read that."

"Okay fine, I'll find some boring celebrity and her diet to write about."

"What am I going to write on?"

"Something will come to you."

Hopefully. Or they would have a newspaper filled with celebrity gossip, princes on holiday and a celebrity's rabbit food diet.

"What am I going to write on?" Kaela sang as she walked around the outside of the beginners' ring, swinging a stick at every syllable.

She had not been able to teach the beginners' class, as Wendy had not seen them ride in a week and needed to correct mistakes the part-time teachers might be missing. Much to Kaela's dismay, Wendy found quite a few mistakes.

"Girls, put your toes in more."

Kaela never remembered to bring her toes in.

"Keep your head forward, even a gentle movement is a shift in balance; you might confuse your horse."

Kaela had let them do whatever they had wanted with their heads.

"Bend your elbows, shoulders back, don't move your hands around so much. Feel the gait of your horse, don't just post and expect the horse to adapt to you."

As much as Kaela hated to admit it, she still had a lot to learn when it came to teaching. She had just assumed that the girls would naturally fix all that on their own.

"If it makes you feel any better, I didn't even notice that their toes weren't in," Angela said, joining Kaela on the fence.

Strangely enough, that did make Kaela feel better. She was just not in the mood to speak to Angela. Would she ever be in the mood?

"Angela, having a mobile so close to my horses is not a good idea, the high-pitched ringing may startle them," Wendy called.

119

Kaela looked over to see Angela with the mobile in her hand. Kaela didn't even bother bringing her mobile to the stables, it had more of a chance of getting trampled than it did of improving her social life. The only thing she missed was having her Jamiroquai ringtone randomly start up at odd moments. There was nothing better than good music surprising you when you were doing something as boring as making a sandwich. Angela obediently turned hers off.

It probably plays nonsense music anyway, Kaela thought.

"I was just asking my mom to come fetch me," Angela explained.

"Why aren't you staying for the meeting?" Wendy said, "Michelle, don't hold your back so stiff. It must be straight, not stiff."

"I didn't know I had to stay, I'm not in one of your classes."

"But you are still a rider here, I expect you to attend the meeting."

"Okay," Angela said. She turned her mobile back on and walked off.

"Amy, pull Caesar back in line, be firm with him."

Caesar's ears shot back and he bared his teeth. No amount of tugging from Amy would bring him back to the line.

"Amy, relax. Relax your grip, relax your shoulders, breathe calmly," Wendy said soothingly.

Caesar relaxed right along with Amy.

"Okay, now take him back to the line."

Amy squeezed with her little legs and pulled on his left rein. As soon as Caesar's head turned he bared his teeth again.

Kaela knew that horses bared their teeth at each other when they were threatening one another. Angela came back to the fence, without her mobile this time.

Amy tried once more to get Caesar to go where she wanted him to go; this time she kicked him instead of just squeezing. He threw his head up and down and tugged at his bit. Little Amy, who was quite a deal smaller than Caesar and not so strong, began to get worried, her face turned red and huge tears fell down her cheeks. Before Wendy could say anything, she dismounted and tried to grab the reins. She could not get a good grip on them and Caesar began bucking. Amy backed away so quickly that she tripped on her own feet and fell into the gravel. Caesar's bucking hooves came closer and closer to the fallen rider.

"Yaaaah!" Wendy cried and clapped her hands in mid-air.

Caesar took that as his cue to exit, he stopped bucking and trotted to the fence where Kaela caught his reins and spoke to him soothingly.

"Shhh Caesar, quiet boy, relax."

She looked over to Amy who sobbed on Wendy's shoulder; the other riders had all stopped to stare at them. Out of the corner of her eye, she could see Angela get up higher on the fence and look around. Soon Pumbaa got tired of just standing and ambled along on his own mission.

Michelle did nothing to stop him. Kaela was about to call out to Michelle to pull Pumbaa back when the bay pony shied at a clump of bushes. Despite Michelle's tugging on the reins he trotted over to the fence, where Kaela grabbed his reins before he could do anything else.

"Be firm with him or he is going to think he is boss," Kaela said to the trembling brunette on Pumbaa's back.

Kaela looked down on the ground where Angela was crouched; she was looking around and moving slightly to the right.

"What are you doing?" Michelle asked before Kaela could.

"Looking for something."

Wendy came up and took Caesar's reins from Kaela, "I think everybody should dismount," all seven girls dismounted without being told twice, "Loosen the girths and take the horses for a walk around the feeding paddock, but be careful around the other horses."

The girls did as they were told; Amy warily came up to Caesar.

"What's wrong with him?" she asked.

"I don't know, but we're going to find out," Wendy said, stroking Caesar's neck.

"I got it!" Angela called from the ground.

Everybody looked at the blonde rider as she raced for the clump of bushes. She dug her hands in and pulled out a black and grey bushbaby with big watery eyes.

"Wow, you're magic," Amy said.

The bushbaby, absolutely terrified to find itself out in the open, hid its face in the crook of Angela's elbow. It looked as though she was carrying a tiny teddy bear. Kaela had never lost the sheer delight that came from seeing a bushbaby or two (or a hundred by that point in her life). They were fluffy and gorgeous, and belonged on a child's bed. This particular one could not have been any older than a month. It put its tiny paws over its ears and tucked its raccoon-like tail between its legs.

"It's so sweet," Amy said, "Can I have it?"

"No, it has been separated from its mother. It needs to be taken to the sanctuary so they can take care of it," Wendy said.

Angela walked up to Caesar with the bushbaby still in her arms, his ears went back and he bared his teeth.

"Caesar's afraid of bushbabies," Amy giggled.

"He has never been this close to one before, he's probably never seen one in his life before," Wendy said.

With a lot of cooing and sweet talk, Angela had Caesar curiously sniffing at the bushbaby in no time. When he was satisfied that the fluff-ball was not a diabolical ploy to destroy the stable from within, he gave an approving nod and turned to see if Amy had any treats.

"So, what are you going to do with it?" Angela asked.

"Get Bart to take care of it until I have time to take it to the sanctuary. Would you mind taking it to him and explaining?" Wendy asked.

"No, I don't mind," Angela said, and walked off.

Kaela minded.

"Do you think you could handle him now?" Wendy asked Amy.

The little rider reluctantly nodded and took the reins. She loosened the girth as Wendy walked off. "Will you walk with me, Kaela?" she asked quietly.

To stop herself from following Angela up to Bart's room, Kaela went with Amy.

"That was bad, I didn't know what to do," Amy confessed.

"You did fine. Riding horses is dangerous; sometimes the best thing to do is to get off," Kaela said.

"But I didn't know that he was just scared. I wouldn't have run away from him."

"The best thing you did was run away," if that hobbling backwards then falling flat could be considered running, "He could have really hurt you."

"But what if he thinks I don't like him because I didn't help him when he was scared?"

Kaela didn't think that a scared horse really cared whether or not a human could help him, but she had to say something to cheer Amy up. Plus, Amy had done something right and needed to be told about it.

"Do you know how I know that Caesar isn't cross with you?"

"How?"

"Because when you jumped off him, you tried to grab his

reins instead of just leaving him. That was a very, very good thing to do, and Caesar knows you did it because you care about him."

That worked, Amy was all smiles until the meeting.

Trixie arrived as Angela walked through the car park carrying something fluffy. She was talking softly to it and stroking it with her index finger.

"Is that a teddy bear?" Trixie asked.

Angela looked up in surprise, "No, it's a bushbaby. We found it in the bushes around the beginners' ring."

"Are you sure its mom wasn't there?"

"Didn't see her. Something must have scared her off."

"What are you doing with it now?"

"Taking it to Bart who is going to keep it until Wendy can take it to the sanctuary."

Trixie raised her eyebrows, "You are taking it to Bart? Kaela is going to kill you."

"I hope not."

Trixie stared at the blonde rider. This was her moment to ask for advice. But did she really want to incur the wrath of Kaela?

"I'm gonna go drop this little one off," Angela said with a smile and turned away.

Trixie watched her walking towards the house, ponytail

swishing, sunglasses pushed to the top of her head, glinting.

"Wait," Trixie cried and ran to her, "You seem to know a lot about dressage. And I have a question."

"Okay," Angela replied slowly.

The two walked towards the house together, "It seems to me that with dressage you have to go as slow as possible. Is this true?"

"Not necessarily. You go at whatever speed you are comfortable with. I think when you are first learning, slow is easier, but once you and your mount learn to work together, you can speed up a bit."

"But what about Felicity Willoughby? She won everything, and she took twice as long to do anything."

"She competed in a side saddle. I would also go at snail's pace. When she was doing more complicated moves and had to use a normal saddle, she moved a bit quicker."

"Did she?"

"At the Empire Games she had one of the fastest times. I think only the saddle and dress slowed her down in other competitions. Also, she invented a move called the 'Felicity's Cross' and I'm doing it at my next dressage competition, she did it far faster than I can. I've just learnt it and she invented it, so of course she was faster. I'll get there."

Trixie nodded, "Don't let Kaela see you doing the Felicity Cross."

"She's seen me. She was watching me on Saturday."

"And she was okay?"

"I guess. Why?"

Trixie sighed, "Felicity Willoughby is Kaela's mother."

Angela stopped and looked at Trixie, her jaw dropped. Then, inexplicably, her eyes filled with tears, "So then she got what she wanted."

"She did?"

Angela nodded, "A daughter who rides big horses."

Trixie was about to say that she didn't fully get what she wanted, as Kaela never did dressage. But suddenly that didn't seem important.

Kaela rode big horses and she always supported Trixie in dressage, despite finding it boring. Wasn't that more than enough?

"So why do you like dressage?" Trixie asked.

"Because it is all about being meticulous and in control. When my life is crazy, dressage makes me slow down and get back in charge. Why do you like it?"

Trixie had never thought about it before, she really had to think about this answer. Finally she said: "Because it's magic."

"Okay everybody, listen up," Derrick said as all the riders gathered around the tables, "As you may or may not know, horse riding isn't exactly the most popular of sports."

Lots of boos greeted this statement.

"It's true: Apley Towers has the lowest amount of riders that it has ever had. And we're not the only ones, both of our deadly rivals – Barren Hollow and Pignut Spinney – are complaining about small classes."

"Well maybe that's because there are three riding schools on the same road, how intelligent is that?" one of the older riders said.

"True, having two riding schools right next to us is probably the dumbest idea in the world, but we were here first. They are the dumb ones. Don't tell them I said that."

"Blackmail material," Trixie whispered into Kaela's ear.

Kaela had only a moment to start worrying about Trixie's ulterior motives before Derrick spoke again.

"So we have decided to bring more attention to all three riding schools, in the hope that this will bring more riders," Derrick continued.

"Are we having a competition against each other?" another advanced rider asked.

"Yes and no," Derrick said, "It will be a competition and it will be against one another, but it's not going to be your average competition."

Derrick smiled at the sea of confused faces before him. It was almost as though he enjoyed it.

"On Saturday, the three schools will be having a scavenger hunt."

Murmurs rose up from the crowd; this would be the first time the schools had ever done anything like this.

A gloved hand rose in the air.

"Yes Bella, something to say?" Derrick asked through clenched teeth. Bella was not Derrick's favourite person in the world, he tolerated her merely because his job dictated it.

"How is that going to bring attention?" she asked.

"I was getting to that," he said hoarsely, "Everybody will be broken up into teams, and a list of the teams will be put in the newspaper for people to bet on, exactly like horse racing."

"They're going to bet on us?" Moira asked, "Is that even legal?"

"Yes," Derrick said gruffly, "Individuals, as well as companies hoping for a batch of free advertising, can bet. Now, it's all perfectly legal and all the money goes to the winners. But Yvonne has offered to hold a food table where she will be selling … ah …" Derrick looked through his papers carefully, "Aah … she hasn't told me what she'll be selling, but Yvonne will have the food table and the profits will come to the stable."

Everybody applauded. Yvonne Everette's daughter rode in the beginners' class, and so Yvonne took that as an open invitation to get as heavily involved in the affairs of the stable as possible, sometimes to the point of getting too involved.

To the detriment of everyone in the vicinity.

"You will be happy to know that Virgo Street will be blocked off to cars and only pedestrians can enter," Derrick said proudly.

Virgo Street was the road outside the stable; it was an

extraordinarily long road with three large stables, a preschool, a garden centre, and a house that belonged to an old man who never left it.

"What about the garden centre?" one of the riders asked.

"They have agreed to close their doors for one day – they are going to use the time to do stocktaking. And in exchange, we will give them as much advertising as possible."

"And old man Henry?" another asked.

"Mr Henry has agreed to let us shut the road down."

"It's not like he ever comes out anyway," Bella said.

"The affairs of another man are not our concern," Warren said.

Warren was a much older rider who Trixie currently had a crush on, Kaela turned to smile at her friend.

"Don't smile at me, you'll give the game away."

"That's right, Warren. Everything is set for Saturday: there are going to be road blocks as well as policemen. And Yvonne has arranged for the policemen to be on horseback."

Everybody laughed: no policeman in South Africa had ever done his shift on horseback. Only Yvonne could have gotten that right. Samantha, Yvonne's daughter, hid her face in her hands.

"The list will be published in tomorrow's newspapers as well as all the details for the scavenger hunt. I'm counting on you to get as many people here as you can. So advertise, advertise, advertise."

"Oh Pan's Pipes!" Kaela cried. Everyone looked at her,

"I can write my article on the hunt. All right people, crisis averted."

Everybody stared at her, someone coughed.

"Right okay, thank you Kaela for that scintillating explanation. I'm glad we could provide a topic for your article. Again. Anyway, moving on," Derrick shook his head and looked through his notes, "I am also expecting every rider here to take part: it's the future of your riding school at stake, so I hope everybody is willing to make a contribution."

Everybody nodded their agreement, including Angela.

"How is the hunt going to work?" Russell asked.

"Every team will be given a list and they have to bring back as many things on the list as they can. The team with the most wins."

"What if there is a tie?" Shanaeda asked.

"I don't know, we'll probably do a tiebreaker – barrel racing or something," Derrick said.

Everybody groaned, barrel racing was a western riding event; all three schools taught English riding.

"Okay, okay, so the event of a tie did not cross our minds," Derrick confessed.

"What kind of organising is that?" Bella asked.

"Keep quiet Bella, they're doing the best they can," Jason said.

Jason was an advanced rider from Barren Hollow, who Bella had not so secretly adored all year. Kaela wasn't sure why a rider from another stable stood in front of the Apley riders, but she relished the look on Bella's face at his retort.

"Thank you Jason," Derrick said, "Jason and the rest of the committee meet again tonight to discuss the queries of the riders. Any queries?"

"How are the teams picked?" Jasmyn asked, with her arm linked through Emily's.

Jasmyn and Emily were one year older than Trixie and Kaela and just as inseparable.

"Unfortunately, teams have already been picked. To get variety in teams, we decided to separate friends and even put riders from different schools in the same team. Every team will be made up of a beginner, an intermediate and an advanced rider."

Kaela heard Trixie's sigh of relief and smiled. Russell was also an intermediate, so they couldn't be put in the same team. As Derrick called out the teams something nagged at Kaela's brain. She knew whatever it was was important, but it danced just beyond her grip, out of sight and out of reach.

"Samantha, Russell and Moira," Derrick called.

That was it, she had it. Too many people shared the same horses: there were not enough horses to go around.

"Kirsten, Bella," everybody groaned, those two in one team would kill the poor advanced rider, "and Jason."

Kaela had never seen Bella with such a big smile.

"She looks like a jack-o'-lantern," she whispered.

"That's why they only let her out of her cage at Halloween," Trixie answered, smirking.

Everybody knew that Jason was probably the only rider on earth that could control the sisters and so it was good that he was put in their team, even if he did come from a different stable. Kaela still felt sorry for him though.

"Shanaeda, Trixie and Warren," Trixie grabbed Kaela's arm and squeezed the life out of it.

"You are giving the game away," Kaela teased.

"Whose team am I going to be on?" Amy whispered to Kaela. There was worry in her eyes.

"I don't know, but at least you don't have to worry about being on Bella's team," Kaela answered.

"Poor Jason," Amy said, returning her attention to Kaela's left hand. She had been playing with Kaela's fingers throughout the whole speech.

"There is only one more team from Apley Towers – the riders whose names I haven't called will be paired with riders from another school, so you are just going to have to come talk to me after the meeting. The last team is Amy, Kaela and Angela."

Kaela's stomach dropped into her feet.

"Tough luck old girl," Trixie said.

"Okay, the rest come see me afterwards. Are there any last minute queries?" Derrick asked.

Kaela's hand shot into the air, nearly taking Amy with it.

"Yes Kaela?"

"There aren't enough horses. How are both Moira and I meant to ride Quiet Fire at the same time?"

"Yeah, both Kirsten and I ride Flight," Emily said.

"I ride Casino, but so does Warren," Jasmyn added.

"Don't worry, we've already sorted that out. There is one extra horse at Barren Hollow as well as one extra horse at Pignut Spinney, they are all retired horses so I want easy riding from you–"

Angela's hand rose before he could finish.

"Yes Angela?"

"I've got two horses, so somebody can ride one of mine. And my grandfather has three retired horses but they are in pretty good shape, I'm sure he wouldn't mind lending them."

"That'll be great, just organise it with him first."

Angela grabbed the famous mobile and wandered off.

"I was going to ask if anybody else knows of horses that we could borrow, but maybe that has already been solved," Derrick said, scouring his list of notes once again.

Angela came back with a cheesy smile on her face, "He says that we can use them with pleasure, but one horse doesn't have a saddle – but don't worry I can take care of that."

Everybody applauded Angela, even Kaela.

"So that is six extra horses. How many of you share horses?"

Twelve hands went into the air.

"Excellent. Okay–"

"Wait a minute," Kirsten said, sounding exactly like her

sister, "Who is going to ride Apley Towers horses, and who is going to ride the old horses?"

"Wendy and I will discuss that tonight. Okay, that's everything done."

The riders strolled off in their own directions. The intermediate class had been cancelled for that day, but Wendy had made it quite clear that she expected clean horses and tack.

Kaela couldn't groom Quiet Fire as he was going to be used in the advanced class, but she thought that he could still use a hug. She wrapped her arms around his neck and buried her face into his mane. His scent was intoxicating; it reminded her of many happy years on horseback.

Kaela could hear that Angela was approaching – every rider she passed thanked her for her contribution. If Kaela had been a braver person, she probably would have thanked Angela as well.

"Hey."

Kaela jumped, she had not expected Angela to stop at her stall. She turned to face her.

"Hey."

"Since we're in the same team and my horses work better together, maybe you could ride Fergie instead of him," she said pointing to Quiet Fire.

"Okay," Kaela said without putting up a fight, she knew she had very little chance of riding Quiet Fire as it was; she might as well take up the offer instead of having to beg for it.

"Have you ever ridden a mare before?" Angela asked.

"I don't think that there is much difference between a mare and a gelding," Kaela said with bite. She forgot that if she became defensive, Angela became just as defensive.

"You've clearly never ridden a mare before," Angela said with equal bite.

Kaela just raised her eyebrows.

"They're more difficult than geldings and they are cheeky, just like human females," Angela said, it was noticeable that she was trying to calm herself down.

Kaela searched her brain, she was positive that she had ridden just as many mares as she had geldings. What she discovered as she went through every horse she had ever ridden, was that there was a serious lack of mares in her past. She could count on one hand the amount of mares she had ridden. Apparently her thoughts had dawned on her face, because Angela was smiling.

"So, not that many mares?" she asked.

Kaela only shook her head.

"So how did those rides go?"

Disastrously, was the only word Kaela could think of. Every mare had thrown her, had not listened to her, had made a complete mockery of riding. She had never gotten along with any mare she had ridden.

"Not good. Why can't I ride female horses?"

Angela laughed before answering; Kaela thought that this was hardly a laughing matter.

"It's not that you can't ride mares, it's that you are used to riding geldings. I mean Apley Towers has hardly any mares."

Kaela looked at the horses in their stalls, all geldings. In fact, all the horses in this row were geldings, all except Fergie and Dawn, and they didn't belong to Apley. Kaela was shocked. Why did Apley Towers have so few mares?

"So what is the difference between a gelding and a mare?" Kaela would never have believed that there was a difference if all her memories had not come flooding back to her.

"It's not a big difference, it's just that geldings are more subordinate – if you want it done they will do it – where mares have enough spirit to make riding a challenge. Not as much spirit as stallions, but that's a completely different story."

Angela's eyes suddenly went wide and she stopped speaking.

Kaela was used to this; in other words, Angela knew who her mother was and believed a stallion had killed her.

To save them both a moment of awkwardness, Kaela changed the subject, "I look forward to riding Fergie on Saturday then," she said.

Kaela thought that it was high time she tested her riding abilities, and was glad for the opportunity.

If not slightly petrified.

Trixie quickly checked LetsChat on her sister's laptop before heading to bed.

She had one notification and a message. It was probably the most popular she had been all year.

"Phoenix White Feather commented on your status," Trixie read. She clicked on the notification and waited for the page to load. She could hear her sister singing softly in the shower.

TK: *Can't wait for Saturday. This is the stuff Jane Austen wrote of.*

Phoenix White Feather: *Abandonment? Self-esteem issues? Slavery and the class divide? Unhappy marriages?*

"No," Trixie quickly hit *comment* and typed a reply.

Trixie King: *I was referring to the love part.*

As usual, Phoenix answered as quickly as lightning. The girls had learned that the school Phoenix attended required the students to work on a laptop instead of books. Therefore Phoenix was on the internet for the majority of her day. It made chatting to her rather easy, although how she got any schoolwork done was anyone's guess.

Phoenix White Feather: *What love? Unrequited? Austen did not write romance, she wrote com-*

plicated arranged marriages with relations, and weird side relationship stories. You want a real romance, read anything by Mary Shelley. She is a sheer genius and deals with love in weird and wonderful ways.

Kaela Willoughby: *Okay, so maybe Mary Shelley writes about 'weird' love. But Trixie's talking about ROMANCE.*

Phoenix White Feather: *Romance should be a man madly in love with a woman who could beat his butt at ANYTHING.*

Trixie King: *Phoenix's dream man isn't all that talented in anything is he?*

Russell Drover: *Maybe he is letting her win because he is a gentleman and he loves her.*

Phoenix White Feather: *That's not love, that's lies.*

Trixie King: *In other words, Phoenix can't be pleased.*

Russell Drover: *What if they were equally matched, each could save the other, and they were together* *because they loved one another, not because they could save the world.*

Phoenix White Feather: *Puke!*

Russell Drover: *You're girls. You should be falling all over yourselves for romance.*

Kaela Willoughby: *Couldn't give a piece of strawberry liquorice about it.*

Phoenix White Feather: *Hmmmmmm … Strawberry liquorice. I would be falling all over myself for a man who brought me strawberry liquorice.*

Kaela Willoughby: *Really?*

Phoenix White Feather: *Probably not, no. I don't even know what to do with a boyfriend. How much does it eat? Am I expected to entertain it? Is it toilet-trained?*

Kaela Willoughby: *No! They lack the ability to put the toilet seat down.*

Phoenix Willoughby: *I already have six brothers to do that.*

Russell Drover: *Trixie! Side with me! Romance is good ... It makes life worthwhile. Right?*

Trixie King: *I'm still dreaming about the strawberry liquorice.*

Melody came into the room, streaming shower mist behind her. The scent of blueberry and cinnamon followed her in.

"Are you almost done?"

"Yup, let me just check this message."

Trixie clicked on the message and was surprised to see Angela's name.

Angela: Hi Trixie,

Here is an interview with Felicity Willoughby about dressage.

I think you might find what she has to say interesting.

Angela

Trixie clicked on the link and waited for the page to download. Slowly but surely, Felicity's face appeared on the screen. The article started off by rattling on about her achievements in the saddle. It then went on to her love of history and why she wore riding habits and used a side saddle, and then the almost Shakespearean serendipity that lead to her meeting – and eventual relationship with – her husband.

Finally, after nearly two pages, the interview started.

Equine Magazine: How has your life changed since winning gold at the Empire Games?

Felicity Willoughby: To be honest, it has not changed much, if at all. I was hardly a celebrity before, and the people who would have recognised me can't because I'm not wearing the Victorian habit.

Equine Magazine: I am afraid to say, that's how I would recognise you.

Felicity Willoughby: That is how most people would recognise me. Although, my life was quite chaotic right after I got back to South Africa because I was invited to interviews and parades, so I felt like a movie star for a tiny portion of my life. But my grandmother quickly put me back in place.

Equine Magazine: How did she do that?

Felicity Willoughby: Well, my husband and I went to her house for lunch, and I asked her if she had seen my winning ride. She said she had missed it because she had to take a nap. That brought me back down to earth rather quickly. My grandmother thought napping was more important than watching me ride in the Empire Games. She keeps me humble when my mother is running around showing off for seventeen hours a day.

Equine Magazine: Your mother makes your Victorian outfits, am I right?

Felicity Willoughby: Yes. It was her idea for me to stand out during a competition. I was fourteen years old the first time she made me a habit. She believed that dressage was boring and I needed to add some excitement.

Equine Magazine: Well, you most certainly don't believe that dressage is boring.

Felicity Willoughby: Not at all. For me, dressage is freedom. In the world you are so bogged down by everything. Everyone always wants a piece of you: you are expected to behave in certain ways and do certain things, and you cannot step off the beaten path. And I used to feel that the world was pulling me in all sorts of directions and I was powerless to find control. Then, when I was fourteen, I began taking dressage seriously, and I learned quite quickly that dressage was one thing

... power! Suddenly, the world was made into a little square, and I was placed in a saddle and expected to command a horse into dancing with me. It took me a few serious falls to realise that once I learned how the horse worked and how to communicate with him, he could help me rule the ring. As soon as I learned that, dressage was my way of ruling my life: I became stronger in everything. When the bullies used to pick on me in high school, all I would think is that I could talk to a horse through my legs, what could they possibly do? I feel the same way now about my critics. I can make a horse dance with invisible aids, all they can do is put pen to paper. And not very well at that.

Equine Magazine: So in the end, what have you been led to believe?

Felicity Willoughby: Dressage is power.

Trixie showered, dressed and got into bed in a daze.

To her, dressage was not about power, simply because she was in awe of it and maybe a little frightened. She was the little girl in the audience while Dressage the Magician pulled a rabbit from a hat. There was nothing powerful about that.

Would she ever feel powerful?

∽ Ten ∾

"Maybe I should set up a table and sell things too," Alice said.

"Go for it. I'm not going to buy anything though, I have no money and you are my grandmother. I should get things for free."

Leo looked at his daughter and shook his head, "You sound like the Mafia."

"I'd make a great Mafia boss."

"I don't doubt it."

The tumble drier inexplicably started up on its own, making all three family members jump.

"Ghosts," Leo said.

"I wish they would do the dishes as well as the laundry."

"Oh, and another thing: Wendy pulled us aside and told us that we need to dress up. That way, even though all three schools are advertising, everyone will only remember the school that dressed up."

"Is she in the Mafia too?" Leo asked.

"What are you going to dress up as?" Alice asked.

"I'm not sure. There really isn't anything I already have. Amy has an Alice in Wonderland outfit that she is wearing. And Angela is going to beg her mother for a riding habit when they go shopping for a saddle, so we have a definite Victorian theme going. Any suggestions on a Victorian outfit for me? Maybe Victoria herself? Dad, I need a crown."

"Start saving."

Alice took a deep breath and said, "Why don't you wear your mother's habit?"

The only sound in the house was the tumble drier. The three family members stared at each other. The air was electric. Dangerous.

"Well, it's been sitting in a box for ten years," Alice argued, "What's the point? Just wear it. It took me a year to make that thing. I had to use a book written in 1818. The first line in the book was, *'Before beginning, acquire your husband's permission'.* I tell you, I wanted to walk up to my husband and whack him on the head for all those women who couldn't do it. And now that dress is sitting in a box." She paused for a moment, "Breaks my heart."

Kaela's heart hammered. Her undigested food slowly crept back up her throat.

Finally, Leo said, "It would be too big."

Alice shook her head, "It has lacing: it can easily be pulled smaller. It may be too long as Felicity was taller, but those dresses were designed to be long. Kaela will be on a horse anyway, the length won't matter. And we could put the sweet little riding cap on her head and curl her hair up and–"

"No," Leo barked, "No."

The pair looked at him.

"No riding cap. She wears a hard hat. Kaela is only ever allowed on a horse with a hard hat. No riding cap. End of discussion. Excuse me."

He pushed his chair back and left the table, taking his almost full plate to the kitchen.

Alice stared at her own plate.

"Was my mother wearing a hard hat the day she went out riding and never came back?"

"No," Alice said quietly.

Would things be different if she had been?

The next week was spent preparing the riding schools for the hunt. Some of the riders were coming out in full Empire Games uniform to mimic the look of the aristocracy on a fox hunt. Trixie had told her team that she thought the idea was just plain cruel: why would you want to glorify a cruel tradition that had been outlawed before she had even been born?

Trixie hadn't given her outfit much thought. She never did. But she had put her foot down at the suggestion of her team dressing like fox hunting aristocrats. She would sooner wear a clown outfit on horseback.

Tuesday's private dressage lesson proved Felicity wrong; there was nothing powerful about dressage. There was just pain and danger. Not only were Bella and Trixie expected to ride without reins, but now their stirrups had been taken away. Trixie had managed to stay on the horse, but only barely.

The two girls took their horses on an outride, but both were practically asleep in the saddle. Neither girl said anything to the other. Trixie preferred it that way.

"Hey, Trix!"

She begrudgingly turned to the owner of the voice only to find Warren on horseback coming down the lane behind the girls.

"Hi," she squeaked.

He smiled at her and she wondered where her knees had gone (not that she hadn't been wondering the same thing since halfway through her lesson).

"I have an idea for dressing up: how about horror characters? I have a Dracula outfit, and my little sisters have lots of witchy stuff lying around."

Trixie smiled, she was so happy he had come up with a good idea and she hadn't been forced to tell her crush that his plan sucked, "I like it!"

The two made plans to get the outfits off him and get one to Shanaeda before Saturday, he then bid them farewell and returned to the stable. Trixie watched him trot off.

Bella began laughing, "You wish!"

Trixie rolled her eyes, but she had no energy to reply.

Kaela watched as Alice punched the numbers into the padlock. Her birthday. That left her cold.

The lock clicked open and Alice pulled it off. She pushed the heavy steel lid up and pulled out the Victorian habit. The dust on it was ten layers thick, even though it had been locked up in a steel chest. One layer for every year in the dark.

Kaela tried to breathe. She couldn't.

That had been the dress to go with Felicity whenever she won gold. That was the dress in all the press photos of Felicity.

She closed her eyes, she didn't want to deal with it.

"We'll have to send it to the dry cleaners," Alice said as she tried to dust it off, "I don't trust the washing machine."

Kaela followed her grandmother out of the loft and down to the kitchen. The dress was like a black hole, sucking every molecule out of her body. She couldn't look at it, but then she also couldn't look away.

"I'm going to get my shoes and then we can take it into town and see about getting it done pronto," Alice said and walked off.

Kaela stood next to the counter and stared at the habit. It lay straight, as though the ghost of Felicity was sleeping.

She slowly stepped forward and touched it. The heavy velvet shocked her. She ran her fingertips up from the skirt and onto the bodice, where black embroidered flowers decorated the corset. She could feel the steel ribs under the fabric.

It was most certainly authentic. But then again, Felicity's father had been a historian.

Kaela pinched the blue velvet between her fingers. She tried to separate the dress's last owner from the current situation.

She imagined herself in the saddle, on a horse, in the sunlight. How did she feel?

Powerful.

The Victorian era was the first time that women were not only allowed to step out of the shadows, they were actually encouraged to.

Is that why Felicity wore the habit with such pride? Because she was stepping out of the shadows and into the limelight, and taking the rest of South Africa's female riders with her?

Was she fearless, and therefore, powerful?

Kaela gripped the steel ribs and imagined how she would feel in the saddle.

Fearless, therefore powerful.

⚜ Eleven ⚜

On the day of the hunt, Trixie received the fright of her life. Dressed as a witch complete with hat, spiderweb dress, and purple and black striped stockings, she hopped out the car and waved her mother and sister goodbye. She was wearing witch-like heels – not very high, but higher than she had ever worn on horseback. She figured that if Felicity could win the Empire Games in Victorian high-heeled boots, she could win – or at least, participate in – a scavenger hunt. As she adjusted her hat and looked around, her heart stopped beating. Walking towards Trixie with sunlight and shadow making her glow, was Felicity Willoughby in her blue Victorian habit.

Goosebumps erupted across her hairline. She couldn't breathe. She had always believed in ghosts, but she had no idea what she would say to one.

Finally, she blurted out, "How does dressage make you powerful?"

"It doesn't, it makes me bored."

It was Kaela. There was no ghost of Felicity, it was simply Kaela in her mother's dress.

"I thought you were someone else."

Kaela frowned, "You look like you have seen a ghost."

Trixie laughed nervously. She was very glad when the girls were given the instruction to start tacking up.

Virgo Street was abuzz with activity, three schools worth of horses and riders decorated the streets as well as many spectators, food and other nick-nack tables, and a table of insurance salesmen. Which was odd, since horse riders were never insured – it was too risky.

There were big yellow road blocks at each end of the road, and horse jumps had been placed at other entrances to the street.

Trixie adjusted her hat, she couldn't wait to get started.

Kaela sat tall atop Fergie. It had been years since she had last ridden a Thoroughbred. So far riding a mare had been easy, but then again, Fergie was flawlessly trained. Amy, dressed as Alice (she even had a miniature White Rabbit and Cheshire Cat hooked to her skirt) sat on a perfectly well-behaved Caesar. Angela, wearing her brand new black and white Victorian habit, was on Dawn. Of course, her expensive sunglasses were over her eyes. Except for the shoes, hard hats and tack, the girls looked as though they had stepped out of a Dickensian novel.

Kaela did not fail to notice that Dawn had a new saddle on; her old saddle adorned the back of one of the retired horses.

"Riders, if you would please gather around me. Thank you," James, the owner of Barren Hollow, called.

"Is everybody ready?" James called to the mass of riders around him.

Cheers erupted from the crowd.

"Good. It's nice to see so many smiling faces here, as well as so many people to watch the people with smiling faces," James paused for effect. Nobody laughed. It was okay, James always laughed at his own jokes anyway.

"August and January! What a coincidence."

Angela and Kaela looked down: the shirtless rider from Pennylane stood staring up at them. Neither girl said anything. Neither girl could say anything.

"I'll have you know that I am betting on your team, and I hate losing. Here you go little one," he said, and handed a piece of paper to Amy. He gave the girls one last smile and walked off. Kaela was sure she heard him greet Bella with, 'Hello April!'

"At least he had a shirt on this time," Angela said.

Before Kaela was expected to answer, she turned to Amy. "What's that?"

Amy passed it across to her. It was a list of things they had to find in the scavenger hunt.

"Okay riders, here are the rules," James called, "you have to collect as many of the things that are on the list as you can and then bring them back to the judges' table. No one can leave the perimeter of Virgo Street. No one can get a spectator to get things for them. If you get off the horse to retrieve something, you have to get straight back on. All three schools as well as the preschool can be wandered onto, but the garden centre and Mr Henry's house are out of bounds: any rider caught there will be disqualified. Also, nobody is allowed to sabotage anybody else."

"Sorry Bella," one of the boys from Pignut Spinney called. All the other riders laughed. Bella had once purposely fed his horse before a competition so that the horse would not jump. It had all been for nothing as both Trixie and Kaela had still beaten her.

"Quiet down now! Okay, where was I? No rider shall sabotage another rider. No teams will help one another, and no fighting – settle disputes like decent human beings."

"Well that leaves Bella out," another rider from Barren Hollow called.

She had once screamed at him until her face turned blue because he had apparently distracted her during a jump, causing her to fall.

"Come on guys, I want to finish up here before I grow a long white beard," Jason said.

Everyone automatically stopped laughing.

"Thank you, Jason. Well you all know the rules: first one

with everything or the one with the most wins. Go!" the word was barely off James's lips before everybody kicked their horses into action.

Unfortunately all horses were facing one another and the resulting equine knot was enough to drive the bravest pedestrian away in a dishevelled run.

"That Bella sounds like a tyrant," Angela said.

"She is, she once yelled at me at camp for putting my tent too close to hers," Amy said.

"Yeah, but the proximity made it easier to egg her the next morning, so wasn't it worth it?" Kaela asked.

For a moment, you could see the woman that Amy would become: strong, indefatigable and willing to stand up for what was right. And then it was gone and only a little girl smiled and nodded.

"So what's on the list?" Angela asked.

Kaela read everything from the list:

1. A discarded bird's nest
2. A black feather
3. An old horseshoe
4. Three perfect acorns
5. A perfectly round stone
6. An old key
7. A rusty nail
8. A white rose
9. An object from a princess

10. A hare from the back of a Pegasus

"What?!" Angela yelled.

"Where are we going to find a princess?" Amy asked.

"Where are we going to find a Pegasus?" Kaela asked.

"Mum, I'm not riding with you," Bart yelled.

The three girls turned to see Wendy leading Mouse over to Bart.

"Yes you are, now mount – we have a scavenger hunt to win," Wendy said firmly.

"Mum, I have a reputation to protect," Bart argued, he looked thoroughly perturbed and rather hot around the collar.

"Won't you risk your reputation for the sake of the schools?" Wendy asked sweetly.

"No, I can't be seen taking part in a scavenger hunt with my mother. Do you know what the seniors do to boys who hang out with their mothers? They probably have a toilet reserved just for us. Do you want my head dunked in an especially reserved toilet?" his face was turning red and he was even stamping his foot. Mouse appeared to be grinning at him.

"Come on, I don't think it's that bad. Björn is taking part."

Björn sat proudly on Liquorice. Kaela had to laugh at the loose-fitting chaps and hard hat that kept slipping down over his eyes. It was obvious that his outfit had been assembled the night before.

"Björn is not your son, it doesn't matter if Björn rides with you," Bart argued.

"Considering I've lived here every weekend and school holiday since I was nine, I'd say that I'm practically her son," Björn added.

"Thank you Björn," Wendy said lovingly. "Now get on the horse" she said to Bart, not so lovingly.

He reluctantly took the reins and mounted, "I hope this doesn't follow me to university," he moaned.

"If it does, I'm sure they will have an especially reserved toilet there as well," Wendy said, and trotted off.

"Okay then," Kaela said, turning back to her team, "Let's win this hunt."

The first item they found was a nest, they found that under the trees at Pignut Spinney. Amy's mother had saved the day by installing an empty backpack on her daughter's back. The girls used that to carry everything. They had found the perfectly round stone in the fish tank outside of the garden centre. They didn't consider this as disobeying the rules as it was outside the garden centre, not in it. They found the acorns and feather by the trees in the feeding paddock at Apley Towers.

"Too bad we can't get into the garden centre, we'll find a lot of roses there," Kaela said.

"It's summer, there have to be roses somewhere," Angela said.

But the only flowers the girls could find were cosmos, lots and lots of cosmos.

"Why are there so many of these flowers?" Angela asked in frustration.

"They're weeds, they grow wild," Amy said.

"Pretty weeds," Kaela added.

"Forget the rose, princess and Pegasus for a moment, what else do we need to find?" Angela asked.

Kaela looked at the list, "All that's left is an old horseshoe, an old key, and a rusty nail. They're not really all that demanding are they?" Kaela asked, her voice dripping with sarcasm.

She looked at her teammates: both girls had a look of serious concentration on their faces, and then both girls suddenly broke out into a smile.

"Am I missing something here?" Kaela asked, thoroughly confused.

"I know where we can find the nail," Amy said.

"I know where we can find the horseshoe and key," Angela said.

The girls decided to get the nail first; they followed Amy to Caesar's stall.

Amy jumped down, and pointed to a white glob just outside of the stall.

"What is it?" Kaela asked.

"Come see," Amy answered.

The two girls dismounted and looked at the glob. It was children's playdough pressed in against the wall. Kaela reached across and pulled it off: stuck at an odd angle was a very old nail.

"Pan's Pipes!" Kaela cried.

"That is so dangerous," Angela exclaimed.

"I know. Derrick was meant to fix it this weekend, but he couldn't because of the scavenger hunt." Amy said. "That's why I put playdough over it, so that none of the horses could cut themselves on it," she gave them both a lopsided smile.

The older girls stared at Amy in amazement.

"Well done," Angela said proudly.

Kaela laughed at Angela's new favourite saying.

"I need to get something to pull the nail out, I'll be right back."

Kaela grabbed the long skirts, lifted them up and ran into the tack room: the farrier always left a spare hammer here in case he forgot to bring his.

Which Kaela thought was slightly odd seeing as it was the farrier's job to bring a hammer.

It was kept on a shelf in the tack room. Kaela grabbed it and ran back to her team. With the hammer's claw, she ripped the nail out of the wall and threw it into the backpack. She then returned the hammer to the tack room and ran to the car park; she was going to meet her teammates at Angela's mother's car.

When she got there, Angela already had the door open and was digging around inside. She climbed out holding a broken key in one hand and a worn horseshoe in the other.

"How?" was all Kaela could say.

"This key broke ages ago and nobody has bothered to

throw it away, and Fergie got new shoes yesterday, all four of her old shoes are still in the car."

"Well done," Amy said with a huge, toothless grin.

Angela's smile was so big it looked as though the top of her head was going to come off.

"Okay, we'll kiss and hold hands later, right now we should finish the hunt," Kaela said.

"What are we missing?"

"A rose, a hair and an object from a princess."

"Well we can't find a rose, I doubt we are going to find a Pegasus, and we're very far away from the nearest princess," Angela said.

Just then Shanaeda, Warren and Trixie trotted past. Trixie waved, Kaela waved back, then realisation hit her.

"A princess! A princess! There is a princess here," Kaela said and ran back to the stables with a trotting Fergie behind her. The two girls followed her.

"What do you mean?" Angela asked.

Kaela threw Fergie's reins at her and ran back to the tack room. All private owners kept their tack and other equipment in their own personal lockers; Kaela ran for Bella's locker, grabbed what she needed and ran back out.

"Okay, explain," Angela asked.

"Bella is a princess."

Amy snorted.

"No really, she is. Trixie calls Bella 'Princess' to mock her. And Bella knows that Trixie calls her 'Princess'. Therefore she is a princess and I stole her crop," Kaela said, holding the purple crop in front of them.

"Well mark that off the list," Angela said, and remounted. They had already been off the horses too long.

"Now we have to find a Pegasus," Amy said.

Kaela took the note out of her pocket and read it again in case she had missed something. That was when she noticed something very peculiar. She read the words, then read them again, and then really examined them. She smiled a jack-o'-lantern smile when she saw the words clearly.

"What are you smiling at?" Angela asked.

"It's a *hare,* not a *hair.*"

Angela just shook her head.

"It's spelt H-A-R-E, as in the animal; hair – as in hair from your head – is spelt H-A-I-R. They don't want a hair from the back of a Pegasus," Kaela said, grabbing her own long brown hair and shaking her head, "They want a hare from the back of a Pegasus."

"Like the tortoise and the hare?" Amy asked.

"Exactly!" Kaela cried.

"Wait, that makes absolutely no sense. How can you get a rabbit from the back of a flying horse? It's just not possible," Angela argued and folded her arms.

"You clearly haven't been in Wendy's house," Kaela said.

"Anything?" Warren asked.

"No," Shanaeda said. A black spiderweb had been painted across her face, her usually lovely face now appeared rather menacing.

They were looking for a nest. But they were too late. The discarded nests had been picked clean. Barren Hollow was a lot smaller than Apley Towers, with only two riding rings and no practice ring. It didn't take them long to get through the entire property. And come up empty-handed.

"There!" Shanaeda screamed.

Warren and Trixie looked down a tiny alley between two brick walls. On the floor sat a nest. The three looked up. In the branches hung a beautiful green and brown nest, which swung in the wind. The one on the ground must have been the male bird's first attempt at a family nest. If his wife wasn't happy with what he presented, she simply broke it down and he had to start all the way from the beginning again. All South African males were glad they were not birds.

"We won't be able to get it," Warren said.

"Why not?"

"That space is too small, we won't be able to turn the horse around."

The idea of getting off the horse to walk there was ludicrous to them. A scavenger hunt on horseback meant you took the horse with you.

"Wait," Trixie said, an idea forming in her head, "I can do it."

She nudged Slow-Moe forward into the alley. When he was almost at the nest, she halted him. It was too tight to get off by his side so Trixie kicked her foot loose of the stirrup and swung her leg over; she hung it over the pommel, as if she were sitting side saddle. Staying as close to Slow-Moe's neck as possible, she slid down and landed with a soft thud next to his head. She quickly leaned down and grabbed the nest. Getting back on was harder. She put her hand against Slow-Moe's stomach and gently pushed him towards the opposite brick wall. He stepped sideways, almost as though he was doing 'Felicity's Cross'. Trixie now had enough space to put her foot in the stirrup. Although, there was nowhere near enough space to swing her leg over, she simply used the wrong foot, placed it in the stirrup and pushed herself up. She now faced the back of the horse – balancing in mid-air. She slowly pulled her free leg across the saddle, and turned around. There was no space for her leg on the other side so she kept both legs on one side and sat as though she rode a side saddle. Because she was holding the nest, she only had one hand free. She gently took the reins and pulled them towards her stomach. Because Slow-Moe was in a stationary position, he understood that this meant something else was expected of him. She gave slight pressure with her calf and leaned back.

"Come on, Slow-Moe, you can do it," she said softly.

Slowly, Slow-Moe put a hoof back, and then another, and then another until he was quite comfortably walking backwards. As soon as they were free of the constricting alley, Trixie swung her leg over and sat astride him.

Warren and Shanaeda looked at her, brows knitted and mouths hanging open, as though they should be crowning her their queen.

And suddenly, she understood how dressage made you powerful.

Kaela snuck into Wendy's house. It was on the other end of the property, far away from the actual school. Kaela walked through the bright kitchen, through the dining room, and stopped at the foot of the stairs.

"Hello?" she called: she didn't want anybody to catch her snooping around.

When no answer came, she climbed the stairs quickly. At the top of the stairs was a cupboard that came up to Kaela's waist. Decorating the top of the cupboard was a porcelain Pegasus, and behind the Pegasus was a family of wooden hares. There were usually five of them, now there were only two.

"Somebody else knows about the hare from the back of the Pegasus," Kaela frowned.

Once she had the hare she raced out of the house and joined her team.

"Okay we've got nine, we're just missing the rose," Kaela

said as she put the hare in the bag. She looked around the garden but there were only red roses.

"At least nobody will lose their head," Kaela said as she mounted.

Amy looked at her with big eyes.

"I beg your pardon?" Angela said.

"In Alice in Wonderland, the cards have to paint the white roses red or the queen will cut off their heads. All the roses here are already red, nobody is going to lose their head," Kaela explained and smiled.

"Too bad, we kind of need a white rose," as she said that, Angela's eyes got big and a small smile crept onto her face. "Somebody is going to lose their head."

"What do you mean?" Amy asked timidly.

Angela pointed to the next door garden where white roses grew in the hundreds.

"No!" Kaela yelled before Angela could suggest anything.

"Why not?" Angela asked.

"That is old man Henry's garden. We'll get disqualified. We've already won, why do you want to disqualify us right before we get the award?" Kaela asked, shaking her head.

"We'll only get disqualified if we get caught."

"And you don't think there is going to be somebody watching?" Kaela asked. She was more scared of old man Henry than she was of being disqualified. Apley Towers riders had had run-ins with him before; they were never pretty.

Angela had moved Dawn over to the wall, she was reaching over to get a rose, but her fingers only brushed them. Kaela brought Fergie over to the wall, but she could also only just touch them.

"We are going to have to go over the wall."

"Are you nuts?" Kaela demanded.

"I'll climb over, pick the rose and climb back," Angela said.

"You can't climb back over: there is nothing to stand on over that side. Not to mention you will break your neck with those long skirts."

"So then I'll have to jump."

"Now I know you're nuts," Kaela said.

"What about down there?" Amy said, pointing further down the wall, "there are trees, so he won't see you."

Before Kaela could say anything, Angela trotted over. Kaela followed her. Amy followed her.

"She's right, look how shaded it is, he won't see. I'll jump her over, dismount, pick a rose, jump back," Angela said.

"Let me jump, Fergie's legs are longer, she'll fly over this wall," Kaela said. It was a high wall and Dawn was a small horse.

Angela shook her head, "You'll never get Fergie to jump, she hates jumping. Besides, Dawn was born to fly." She patted Dawn on the neck, turned her around, cantered her away from the wall, then came back around to face the garden. She kicked Dawn and the horse galloped, lifted her front feet, and propelled herself skyward. Angela had been right, Dawn really could fly. The little horse tucked her front feet beneath her body and soared over the wall. Kaela noticed that Angela did something rather odd when she jumped. Her left hand lay flat against Dawn's neck instead of being curled around the reins. Angela landed, sprang out of the saddle, raced for a rose bush, picked one and raced back. She sprang into the saddle and was back over the wall in record time.

"I'd officially call us the winners," she said breathlessly.

Amy and Kaela applauded her.

"Now, let's get back before someone sees us here," Kaela said glancing around. The girls cantered away from the houses and only slowed to a walk once they were back with the other competitors wondering amongst the rings.

"Should we tell them we cheated?" Amy asked.

"Shush!" the older girls hissed.

"Well, we did!"

"No we didn't. James said that old man Henry's house was out of bounds. He didn't say anything about his garden," Kaela explained.

Angela laughed and agreed.

Kaela looked at her, if she hadn't just seen Angela jump a five foot wall in a Victorian riding habit, she would have laughed at anyone who suggested it. Kaela wondered if she was staring at the future of riding. Had her mother's legacy come to an end? Was Angela the next to be the face of South African, woman riders?

Had Felicity still been alive, would she have been happy to pass her crown down to Angela?

"Did it make you feel powerful to jump that wall?"

Angela shrugged, "It was just a wall."

"Why do you do that? You downplay what you are good at. Do you think anyone else in the world would shrug off a jump over a five foot wall in a *dress*?"

"It's a habit," Amy corrected.

Angela looked at her with big eyes, "I guess I downplay it so that people don't feel bad."

"Who cares? Sorting out their emotions is not your job. As long as you are not a jerk, it is not your responsibility to make sure everyone else is happy and comfortable. Do you honestly think my mother would have shrugged off something that amazing?"

"No way," Amy cried, "I saw an interview with her where some journalist told her she was lucky to win against males. She told him that she won because she worked her butt off: luck had nothing to do with it. My mom watches that interview whenever she needs to feel powerful. Or my dad bugs her."

Kaela turned and looked at Angela, "See? Even Amy, who wasn't even born when my mom was alive, knows what she would think. Now, keeping in mind how you are supposed to behave when you do something amazing, did jumping that wall make you feel powerful?"

Angela looked back at the wall and down at her long

riding habit, "Definitely, I'd love to see anyone else do that."

Amy laughed, "They couldn't."

Angela looked at Kaela, "Does that outfit make you feel powerful?"

"No," Kaela said quickly. She refused to talk about how it made her feel. She wasn't ready to deal with it.

"Then why did you suggest that you should be the one to jump?"

Kaela smiled at Angela, "Because when it comes to jumping, I am fearless."

"Powerful?"

Kaela nodded, "I am queen of the world."

"What am I?" Amy asked.

"You make a pretty good Alice," Angela told her.

Yes, Kaela thought, *Felicity would be more than happy to pass her crown to Angela.*

Minutes later, the girls triumphantly placed all the findings on the judges' table.

"What's this?" a judge asked, picking up the crop.

"An object from a princess," Amy said proudly.

"I don't understand," the judge said.

"Well, my friend has nicknamed one of the Apley Towers riders: she calls her 'Princess'. This is her crop. So it is an object from a princess," Kaela explained.

"Hey, you stole my crop," Bella cried in the distance.

"And this?" another judge said, picking up the wooden hare.

"It's a hare from the back of a Pegasus," Angela said.

Kaela quickly explained the story behind the item.

The judge shook his head in wonder, "Well I guess that means you are our winners. Congratulations!"

The three girls jumped into each other's arms and hugged each other.

One of the judges got on the loudspeaker and ordered the riders to come back.

Ten minutes later, all the riders as well as the spectators gathered in front of the table.

"Ladies and gentlemen, I would like to announce our winners," James called, "they were the first team back with all of the items, though who knows how they managed the last two! The junior rider is Amy Hanscom on Caesar, the intermediate rider is Kaela Willoughby on Fergie, and the advanced rider is Angela May on Dawn. Give them a round of applause."

Kaela could still hear the whistling and cheering later that night as her grandmother helped her take the habit off. Alice then laid it on the bed and inspected it for any damage.

Kaela hadn't allowed herself to think about what she was wearing but now, with the blue velvet phenomenon lying across her bed, she wondered if it had brought some of her mother's magic to the scavenger hunt.

She stroked the black embroidery on the sleeves and imagined her mother wearing it, winning in it, passing it down, helping Kaela put it on, celebrating her win at the stable.

A painful wish, nothing more. That dress lay empty on

the bed. It was going back in the chest and it wouldn't see the light of day again for years, if ever.

Kaela went to shower, and for the first time since her grandmother had taken it out of the chest, she cried.

She hoped her mother had seen her win in that habit, and she hoped her mother was proud.

❧ Twelve ❧

"So, what are we doing on Saturday?" Trixie asked.

Kaela looked over at her friend. Trixie wore the same smile that had been on her face since the scavenger hunt. Spending one full day with Warren seemed to warrant a full five days of smiles. The girls were walking their horses after a strenuous lesson. The road used for outrides was a dirt road that ran between two plots. Cars and motorbikes were forbidden on it, and this left the horses and riders free to relax and enjoy the scenery. Dark pine trees hung over the road, giving it a shady, enchanted look. Kaela loved living in South Africa, where the ancient trees stretched for miles and anything manmade had no choice but to respect that. In South Africa, the trees are the giants – man is simply allowed to live in their presence. A family of meerkats skittered across the road. The pups stopped to stare at the riders but were hurried on by a nip from their father.

"I actually wanted to go watch Angela compete this weekend," Kaela said shyly.

"In dressage?" Trixie asked hopefully.

"Yes, but also jumping."

"Okay, yeah."

"Hey, you two. I'm riding this weekend too you know," Russell said, nudging Vanity Fair into a trot to catch up with them.

"How about we make it a big thing on Saturday, get the whole stable together to go watch you guys compete?" Kaela asked Russell.

"Sounds like a plan," Russell said.

"How 'bout it Trixie?" Kaela asked, "Want to get everybody together and we go watch them compete?"

"Definitely."

Kaela was willing to bet her new chaps that Trixie had just made Russell's year.

"You never told us how riding a mare went," Russell said.

"You know, I didn't even notice I was riding a mare."

"I think that means you can handle all horses now," Trixie said.

"Except stallions," Russell said.

Trixie shot him a look of death.

"Actually, I learnt to ride on a stallion," Kaela said as she stared at the clouds over the Indian Ocean. They seemed to touch the waves, where a school of dolphins raced the surfers, weaving around them and jumping over the boards,

"A gold medal winning Empire Games stallion."

"Black Satin?" Russell asked warily, holding back his interest.

Kaela smiled at the ocean, "Black Satin. He taught me nearly everything I know."

Suddenly, Kaela had an unbelievable need to ride that beautiful horse in her mother's Victorian riding habit.

And who knew, maybe even do some dressage.

✎ Thirteen ❧

On Saturday, half the riders from Apley Towers made an appearance at Equestrian International. They decided to eat a picnic-style lunch and spread blankets beneath the oak trees just outside of the main riding arena.

Equestrian International was located in one of the wealthiest areas of South Africa. Kaela couldn't even afford to go window shopping there, let alone real shopping.

Kaela gazed across the land. There were riding arenas as opposed to riding rings, they also had *individual stables* instead of stalls, and a '*Royalty Corner*' where the most expensive horses in South Africa resided. The riding college was far from the little riding schools that Kaela was used to: Equestrian International was an academy for serious riders and even more serious riding. Even the name – Equestrian International – showed how exclusive the school was. So much so, that when they had competitions, riders had to be personally invited. Equestrian International also made it a point to only invite people who owned their own horses. At first, Kaela had thought that this was an arrogant move, as the stable was missing out on a lot of talent. But Wendy had explained that they could only invite private owners because using other schools' horses would disrupt those schools' lessons. Kaela had warmed up to the Academy after that: there was a beating heart somewhere inside its fancy exterior.

They couldn't have had a better day for their picnic. The sky was an endless ocean-blue, dotted with marshmallow clouds shaped like winning horses. Kaela lay down with her hands behind her head, closed her eyes and breathed in the excitement of the day. She could hear riders and announcements and, most importantly, the soft whinny of contented horses. The scent was intoxicating: the hot sun beat down on the grassy Midlands, reminding her of summer adventures. In the midst of winter, Kaela sometimes thought of that scent and ached for moments just like this.

"One day I will write all about this," she said.

"We know," the rest of the group cried.

"What did we bring to eat? I'm starving!" Trixie cried, diving into the food basket and knocking Kaela out of her daydream at the same time.

"It's ten in the morning," Moira said.

"And you ate in the car," Emily said.

"And you ate just before we left," Jasmyn said.

"I'm a growing girl," Trixie defended.

"Hi guys," Russell said, walking up to them.

He was dressed in cream breeches, knee-high boots and a black riding jacket. It made his dark skin and eyes a picture of delight. Kaela was amazed that Trixie didn't go weak at the knees, all the other girls had.

"Good luck Russell," everybody chorused.

"We're crossing fingers," Moira said.

"And thumbs," Amy yelled.

"And little toes," Kaela yelled.

"Thanks, it feels good to have support," Russell said and smiled, before glancing swiftly at Trixie and making his exit.

Kaela shot a glance at Trixie, she stuck her tongue out between bites.

The competitions went well, with Apley Towers taking red and yellow ribbons. Finally it was Angela's turn to ride.

"Angela May riding From Dawn until Dusk," a voice called over the loudspeaker.

Angela's supporters cheered and whistled as she came into the ring. Angela looked around, her confused face broke out in a smile as she realised who was cheering her on. She brought Dawn to the starting post and gave a quick wave, everyone waved back.

"Fifteen-year-old Angela May riding seven-year-old From Dawn until Dusk. Angela is the last jumper in this competition, in order for her to win she will have to get through the course with no faults," the voice over the loudspeaker said.

Kaela looked out over the course; it was difficult, she would admit. She didn't think that she would be completely capable of jumping it herself. The jumps themselves were not that threatening compared to the wall Angela had jumped the week before, though. Compared to that, this would be child's play. Kaela was sure that Dawn would fly over them.

The horn blew and Angela kicked Dawn into action. They took the first jump perfectly; they did the second jump even better, and then the third. Angela took Dawn into a large half circle and took the fourth and fifth jump; they then rode around the second jump to take the sixth jump, which was a series of three pops. Kaela knew that Angela would take the combinations with her previous flair and she was right, Angela and Dawn flew over the jumps so quickly that it looked as though Dawn's hooves hadn't even touched the ground. Angela then brought Dawn around for the next jump. She was now facing her audience, Kaela expected to see excitement, or at least concentration, on Angela's face, but what she saw was disappointment and worry.

Does she think she's done something wrong? Kaela thought.

So far Angela had made no mistakes, not even simple ones like forgetting to put her toes in. The only thing that could be held against her was her flat hand on Dawn's neck.

Why does she look so worried? And disappointed? Kaela thought.

Angela took the seventh jump perfectly and brought

Dawn in another large half circle for the eighth and final jump.

"If she clears this jump, she's won," Emily whispered, holding her hands over her mouth.

Dawn cantered to the jump, lifted her front hooves at exactly the right place and propelled herself forward. First her front feet went over the jump, then her midsection, then Angela flew over Dawn's head and landed on the ground with a loud thump. She rolled out of the way, to give Dawn space to land.

The crowd gave a loud 'aahhh' in disappointment.

"What happened?" Amy exclaimed.

"How did she fall?" Emily asked.

Good Question, Kaela thought with a smile.

Kaela appeared to have seen something nobody else had seen.

Angela did not win the competition this time. She kept a low profile for the rest of the day and none of the Apley Towers riders could find her. Despite not winning, Angela had still been the most fantastic jumper there, and the girls, especially Amy, wanted to congratulate her.

It was only much later that Kaela saw Angela go off on her own. She was still riding Dawn and the two were heading for the feeding paddock. Kaela raced for Russell, who she knew was about to untack Vanity Fair and take her home.

"A horse! A horse! My kingdom for a horse," Kaela exclaimed as she came up to Russell. Russell had always been a Shakespeare fan and it was a game between the two of them to quote him. Kaela was probably the only person who would ever play this game with him.

Russell greeted her with a smile, "Is it urgent?"

"It's a matter of saving a rider from herself," Kaela said, panting.

Russell handed her the reins and his hard hat and helped her adjust the stirrups.

"Thank you so much Russell, I'll be back as soon as possible," Kaela said.

"You'd better, the lady wants her supper," he said, pointing to Vanity Fair.

Kaela walked the dappled grey out of the stable. As soon as she was away from the stalls, she kicked Vanity Fair into a canter and raced to catch up with Angela. As Vanity Fair powered across the mammoth landscape that was the feeding paddock, Kaela remembered that she was riding a mare.

There was no fear. There was no fight. She simply rode the horse.

She now understood what her mother had always said to critics … It was not the horse, it was never the horse. What made a ride good or bad, fun or hard work, dangerous or safe, is how dedicated the rider was to communicating with the horse and riding to the best of their ability. Stallion, gelding, mare … It didn't matter, they were all simply horses: it was the rider that was the deciding vote.

Kaela patted her thanks on Vanity Fair's neck.

Angela heard the hoof beats coming up behind her; she turned Dawn and faced the oncoming mare. Her sunglasses, something she hadn't been allowed to compete in, were back on the crook of her nose. Kaela slowed Vanity Fair to a walk and Dawn fell into step next to her.

"I saw what you did," Kaela said.

"What did I do?" Angela asked, without looking at her.

"You pushed yourself off Dawn."

"I did not. I fell, it happens all the time," Angela defended.

"I saw you push yourself. You pushed yourself with the hand that you keep on Dawn's neck. I saw you push yourself off Dawn with that hand!" Kaela stated breathlessly, and pointed quite erratically at Angela's hand.

"Okay, okay I pushed myself off. Big deal," Angela admitted; she was staring intently at Dawn's ears.

"Why did you do that? You would have won," Kaela said.

"And then what? I'd have another trophy and another title for my mother to brag about. Remember when your grandmother said that everybody has to lose so that they see that life does go on? Well, I've just seen that life does indeed go on," Angela explained, looking at Kaela for the first time.

Kaela smiled, she had always done things to test herself and the whole world had always thought she was insane, now here was Angela testing herself and Kaela had thought her insane.

"I didn't even know you were listening to that. But you're right, it's good to lose, it makes you appreciate winning all that much more. But Angela, if you are so good at riding that you always win, I don't think you should sabotage yourself to bring yourself down to everybody else's level. I mean, if you are good, you are good, there's nothing you can do about it except be good. Nobody is going to love you less for being good at something."

"No, they're just going to be threatened by me," Angela spat, halting Dawn.

Kaela halted Vanity Fair and looked at her.

"What do you mean?"

"I mean that everybody is on edge around me, everybody has either got to try to outdo me or they try to make me feel bad for being better than them. And if I try to give them advice, they throw it back in my face," Angela said, close to tears.

She was right, Kaela remembered that Angela had tried to tell Trixie what kind of horse would be best for dressage, and Trixie had gotten defensive. Kaela was willing to bet her new jodhpurs that this was something that happened to Angela a lot.

"You're right. Everybody acts funny around you because

they are threatened and jealous. I know I was. But maybe you should try something different, maybe you shouldn't give advice unless somebody asks for it," Kaela said.

Angela nudged Dawn into a walk, and Kaela followed.

"Do you think that would work?" she finally asked.

"Well look at it this way, you didn't give Amy any advice and now the girl wants to hire you as her own private tutor," Kaela said with a smile.

It was true: since the hunt, Amy would only take horse riding advice if someone pointed out that Angela did it too.

"What were you jealous of?" Angela asked.

"You are my age and you are more advanced than the advanced class. You could get Quiet Fire to jump when I couldn't. You have your own horses. You have a mother who will buy you new tack just because ..." Kaela said.

"Okay firstly, I'm more advanced than the advanced class because they ride for one hour a day; I've been riding for six hours a day every day for the last ten years. You'd be more advanced than them too," Angela argued.

Kaela nodded.

"Secondly, I could get Quiet Fire to jump because I took him over a different jump."

"You couldn't take him over the same jump, it was knocked down," Kaela said, her cheeks burning at the thought of that embarrassing day.

"Even if it wasn't knocked down, I would have taken him over a different jump."

"Why?"

"Because sunlight was bouncing off something, and whenever he went

up to that jump it caught him in the eye ," Angela said.

"How do you know?"

"Because I brought myself up to his level when I was in line with the jump, and something kept catching me in the eye," Angela said with a nervous smile.

Kaela remembered that Quiet Fire had been fine up until the moment before the jump – apparently when the sunlight flashed in his eye. That was why he didn't jump. Then she remembered seeing Angela crouch on the floor to look through the bushes just before she found the bushbaby that had startled Pumbaa and Caesar. Angela put herself in the place of the horse when something was wrong – that was why Fergie and Dawn behaved so well with her. Angela always knew what was happening in the surrounding areas and used that knowledge to the best of her ability. No wonder she was such a good rider.

Kaela looked over at her in amazement.

"And thirdly, yes I have my own horses but if you had paid more attention to your grandmother, you would know that she is questioning everybody to see if you are ready for your own horse."

"What?" Kaela asked in shock, she had not heard of this.

"She asked Derrick that day she came to fetch you, she asked Sandy at Pennylane, she even asked my mother, and the most my mother knows about horses is that the saddle goes on the back. She doesn't even know how it stays there. So yes I have my own horses, but you'll get there. And lastly, my father and I have been riding together for years without my mother; she's just trying to involve herself in my riding somehow. It's a very wasteful way of including herself, but at least she's trying," Angela said with a smile.

"You should donate your old stuff to Apley Towers, they are always in need of tack," Kaela said.

"I'll do that," Angela answered.

They had come to the end of the feeding paddock so they turned the horses around and walked back. Compared to this feeding enclosure, the paddock at Apley Towers looked like a lunging ring. This land went on forever.

"You should get more involved at the stables. Come on outrides with us, clean tack with us, scrub the horses with us, even muck the stalls with us," Kaela said.

"I'll do that," Angela answered again.

Suddenly Kaela focused on the ever-present sunglasses.

"Okay, what is with the riding glasses? Why do you wear them when you are not on the horse?"

Angela touched the glasses and laughed.

"I have to wear them all the time or I'll lose them. This is my second pair this year."

"But it's only February," Kaela said, aghast.

"Exactly."

The two girls rode in silence for a while, each absorbing

all the information they had just been given.

"You should coach Trixie too, she is dying to rip off your head and peer inside to find out all the secrets of dressage."

"Secrets I learned from your mother."

"And she would have been so proud of that fact."

"And of you."

Kaela nodded.

"Thanks for the advice," Angela said after a while, "I won't give any more pointers until they are asked for."

"Yes, so no screaming to the Fairies that they are really bouncy when they have just started cantering," Kaela joked.

Angela blushed and giggled.

"I'm actually very impressed with the strength of their legs. They've only been riding for such a short while but their legs are so strong already. They said that you taught them," Angela said.

"Yes, they had to learn to grip for a competition that was just between the eight of them, and Trixie and I had to teach them," Kaela said, trying not to show off. Well, sort of trying anyway. At least she wasn't being a jerk.

"Well I'm very impressed. I was also impressed with the way you got them to canter without following each other, it was really cool. You are such a good teacher, you should become a horse riding instructor," Angela said.

"And you are such a good rider, you should not jeopardise yourself," Kaela said.

Angela smiled and looked around the paddock, she

supposed they should get the horses back to the trailers and take them home. Just then she caught sight of a fallen tree.

"Hey Kaela, I'll race you to the tree," Angela challenged.

"On the count of three," Kaela said.

"One … THREE!" the girls cried in unison.

They kicked the horses into a gallop and raced across the feeding paddock. The mares were nose to nose, shoulder to shoulder, the girls were ear to ear.

Although they said they would only race to the tree, both girls decided to jump it. The mares' front hooves left the ground at the right moment, their back legs propelling them up and through the air. Angela and Kaela flew together.

Happy. Powerful. Together.

When they landed, the girls brought the horses to a stop and sat laughing at each other.

Nobody had won, but that was okay.

"You know what Angela?" Kaela asked.

"What?"

"I think we got off to a bad start," Kaela held her hand out, "Hi, my name is Kaela Willoughby."

Angela grabbed her hand excitedly, "Hi, my name is Angela May."

"It's a pleasure to meet you, Angela," Kaela said.

And it was. It really was.

"Angela," Trixie cried as the girls rode up to the horsebox, "I'm so glad to see you!" Mainly she was glad she didn't have to talk to Russell any more.

"You are?" Angela asked in surprise.

"Yes, your dressage competition was *brilliant*."

Trixie didn't care about the jumping. When the whole school had sat on the edge of their seats (or picnic blankets) absolutely riveted, Trixie had her eyes closed remembering the dressage from an hour before. Angela had made Fergie dance and hadn't even shown how she had done it.

Ever since Trixie had made Slow-Moe walk backwards with only one hand on the reins and sitting side saddle, she had had an almost hysteric obsession with learning everything else.

If she could do that, she could do anything.

Angela, still in the saddle with the sun shining behind her, looked down at Trixie and smiled. But she didn't say a word.

"She is not giving advice until expressly asked of her," Kaela interjected.

"Oh, okay," Trixie said, slightly disappointed. *It's probably better that way,* she thought. With Angela's almost superhuman ability to ride, some people may find her advice condescending.

"But," Kaela said, "She is not going to downplay her talents."

"As long as I'm not a jerk," Angela said with a chuckle.

"Good plan," Trixie said.

She was glad the two of them had sorted their issues out. Angela and Kaela were practically the same person. It would have been terrible if they hadn't formed a friendship.

With all the knowledge and skills shared between the three of them, they made each other strong. Where everything else conspired to knock them down, they made each other powerful.

Trixie watched as Angela dismounted and began to untack Dawn. What did she want to ask? What she didn't want to ask would probably be a shorter list.

"Angela, how do you do the 'Felicity's Cross'? How do you do a passage? How do you do everything, and how do you do all this without anyone seeing what you are doing?"

"Good grief," Kaela said, "Angela, I hope you have a year to explain."

"I do," Angela said with a smile, "I have all the time in the world to explain."

❧ Fourteen ❧

"Lost Kodas," Kaela began, "Today we gather to invite a new member."

Trixie lifted her glass of bubblegum milkshake. In Canada, Phoenix lifted her mug of hot chocolate. Kaela, already with a glass of wheatgrass infused with ginger and lemon in mid-air, gestured to Angela that she needed to pick up her chamomile tea (secretly, she was rather impressed with her Angela's rather homeopathic choice of drink).

Angela lifted her tea and looked nervously from one koda to another.

"Sister Angela, you must know what is expected of you. The Lost Kodas are a collection of unbiological sisters who support each other. We celebrate our winnings, we mourn our rejection letters-"

"No, we flush them down the toilet!" Phoenix called.

"Sister Phoenix, do not interrupt me, and do not flush paper down the toilet: you'll block the drain."

"Also, you should hang onto those rejection letters so that when you're famous you can rub them in the rejector's faces," Angela said.

"Sister Angela has bite," a male voice said. Phoenix rolled her eyes.

"Stop interrupting me," Kaela said.

"Hello whichever White Feather brother you are," Trixie said sweetly.

"Stop interrupting me."

"It's Arion," Phoenix said, and faced the laptop towards her twin.

Arion looked up and smiled towards the girls. His long hair fell over his shoulders and a beaded bone choker was strung across his neck. Arion's wrists were filled with leather bracelets supporting beads of every colour and shape.

Out of the corner of her eye, Kaela could see Angela eyebrows raise as she saw him.

"Oh you ain't seen nothing yet," Trixie whispered to her, "There are two older ones that are so gorgeous they can only be considered as gifts to womankind."

As the laptop returned to Phoenix, Kaela thought that she didn't really agree with Trixie on that. Yes, Satyr and Chiron were good to look at, but there was something different about Arion. Almost like he was made of ten different versions of himself and each one stared out through his raven eyes. If still waters ran deep, then Arion was deeper than the Mariana Trench. And he knew it.

"Pie getting cold!" Trixie said and indicated Angela's choice of food.

"Well, if you people would stop interrupting me."

"So go, talk," Phoenix said.

"Don't interrupt me. Okay, Sister Angela do you accept the responsibility of standing with your fellow kodas? Of supporting us? Of celebrating and mourning with us? Of being a true unbiological sister?"

Silence.

"Oh! I'm done, you can talk now."

"Yes, Sister Kaela, I do."

"Sister Angela, do you accept the invitation?"

"I do."

"Welcome to The Lost Kodas."

Phoenix and Trixie cheered.

"You can eat your pie and drink your chamomile tea."

"Why don't you help me?" she asked.

The girls happily tucked in.

"Unfair. What am I supposed to eat?"

"Popcorn!" Trixie and Kaela cried.

"What is my first mission as a koda?" Angela asked.

"To teach me everything you know about dressage," Trixie said.

"To teach me everything you know about jumping," Kaela said.

The girls looked at Phoenix, "To have your mom teach me everything she knows about science."

"Oh trust me, you don't want that. Like the cosmos itself, it never ends."

Conversations turned to the solar system then, and debates about why scientists purposely tried to confuse people with the names of stars, planets and galaxies.

No conclusion was made, and no scientists or Roman Gods were there to defend themselves.

Angela went to sleep with the kodas on her mind. Her dreams were filled with real friends who wanted her advice and appreciated her knowledge and skill.

When she woke up, those friends were still there.

Acknowledgements

Firstly, thank you to the team at Sweet Cherry for this opportunity. Thank you all for working so hard on these books, especially Laurie Parsons, who made the books glitter.

Thank you to friends and family (and friends who are family) for all the help and support you gave me while writing this book. I would be lost without all of you.

And thank you to Angela Fawcett who helped me win a scavenger hunt and inspired a story. You remind me that riding is freedom.

Thank you to my dad who read the first story I ever wrote and paid for riding lessons (and new chaps).

And thank you to Shannon, Kael and Leo Berridge for dreaming my dreams with me.

Thank you to Jamiroquai for allowing me the use of their name.

And lastly, thank you to every horse who has ever carried me and taught me to fly.

An interview with Myra King

Where did your main inspiration for Apley Towers come from?

From my own adventures with my riding friends and our stable. Most of what Kaela gets up to, I did at one point in my life.

Did you ride horses when you were a child? Do you still ride now?

I rode for most of my childhood, both in lessons and pleasure riding with friends. I don't ride anymore as I had a serious fall ten years ago and now it is painful to sit in a saddle for a long time.

Did you have a favourite horse when you were younger? Why?

The first horse to show me attitude was a gelding named Pumbaa, but he also rescued me from what would have been a very sticky situation. He was one of the horses to make a massive impact in my life. Quiet Fire was the horse I rode most in lessons and I fell in love with him from the very first moment I laid eyes on him. He was black and beautiful, and carried me as though I was royalty. It was easy to imagine myself in a fantasy novel on his back. Another adorable horse who I'll never forget is a gelding named Jinky. He was a former champion but retired at our stable and was the first horse I ever jumped with. He taught me to fly.

What has been your best riding experience, and your scariest riding experience?

My best riding experience was riding on the beach in Mexico. I love Native American culture and being able to ride on their beach with the tribe, the way they ride, was magic. My scariest riding experience was when I was eleven and I started riding more advanced horses. The jump was put up to 1m, which I had never jumped before, and the horse bolted forward before I was ready. I lost my stirrups and he was cantering far quicker than I was used to so I nearly fell out of the saddle. I had to grip really tightly with my calves. But it was the first time that a horse had to literally launch himself to get over the jump so it was the first time I was aware of the fact that the horse was flying through the air with me on top of him. I had to grip his neck just to stay on, which means I didn't have my reins to stop him. I ended up having to throw myself off to get myself to safety. I must have accidentally told the horse to turn right though, because as soon as I fell, he turned and I landed up underneath him and he had to jump over me. I still have the scar from where his hoof cut me.

What was it like growing up and riding in South Africa?
It was great to have hot weather for most of the year. Our riding lessons were always done in beautiful sunshine and around lots of nature. The thing I enjoyed most about South Africa was the animals. I grew up with the ability to see elephants, lions and leopards in the wild. I can't say I miss the monkeys though; I was always scared of them. They frequently broke into my house and stole my soap.

How do you come up with all of the different characters in the books?
Some of the characters are based on my friends. A lot of the characters are different facets of my own personality. But a few of them came to me on their own.

Do you have any strange writing habits?
I sometimes have to walk around speaking the character's dialogue out loud. The neighbors know me as the mad writer who holds entire conversations with herself.

Do you have any tips or advice for aspiring writers?
Pay close attention to the world and write about it as much as you can.

Do you have any plans to write more books after Apley Towers?
I'm always writing something.

Coming soon in the series...

Book Four

ISBN: 978-1-78226-280-0

Book Five

ISBN: 978-1-78226-281-7

Book Six

ISBN: 978-1-78226-282-4

Pre-order yours today!